D0175371

Op
1st $20 —

By the same author

RIVER
RUNNERS

A TALE OF HARDSHIP AND BRAVERY

RIVER RUNNERS

A TALE OF HARDSHIP AND BRAVERY

By James Houston
drawings by the author

A MARGARET K. MC ELDERRY BOOK

Atheneum 1979 New York

Library of Congress Cataloging in Publication Data

Houston, James A   1921–
    River runners.

    "A Margaret K. McElderry book."
    SUMMARY: Two young boys, who have been sent into
the Canadian interior to set up a fur-collecting
station, are befriended by a Naskapi Indian family.
    [1. Nascapee Indians—Fiction. 2. Indians of
North America—Canada—Fiction. 3. Canada—Fiction.
4. Adventure stories] I. Title.
PZ7.H819Ri   [Fic]   79–14337
ISBN 0–689–50151–X

Copyright © 1979 by James Houston
All rights reserved
Manufactured by Fairfield Graphics, Fairfield, Pennsylvania
Saddle Brook, New Jersey
Designed by Marjorie Zaum
First Edition

FOR
John Knight,
my godson,
AND FOR
his mother
and father

FOREWORD

The Naskapi, whose name means "wild people," dwell along the treacherous rivers that flow north through the silent boreal forests and the open tundra of subarctic Quebec and northern Labrador. Fewer than two thousand in number, they remain one of the most mysterious tribes in all of North America.

Here is an account based on true events that occurred some years ago when a young Naskapi and his friend joined an inland family in their desperate struggle to survive.

James Houston
Fort Chimo
1978

CONTENTS

RIVER
RUNNERS

A TALE OF HARDSHIP AND BRAVERY

I

Alone on the Ice

ANDREW STEWART HEARD THE EXCITED BEATING OF THE
ship's bell above him on the bridge, then an answering
clang clang clang! from the engine room below. He
heard the ship's twin propellers grind into reverse. That
action set the whole ship shuddering from stem to
stern. Andrew was almost flung from his upper bunk
as the chartered vessel struck something hard. There
was a frightening moment of silence, then shouting
and the sound of running feet.

Andrew leaped down, shook the other clerk awake,
pulled on his clothes and pushed open their cabin door.
Beyond the cold iron deck he could see heavy pack
ice. It was all around them. Andrew, unable to believe that this was summer in the Arctic, pulled up his
parka hood against the sharp wind. Off the bow of
their small ship, beyond the blue teeth of the jagged
ice, he could see a low gray-rock coastline almost naked
of trees. The captain, the ship's engineer and most of

3

the crew were leaning over the rails, peering down at the place where the ship's hull had struck the ice.

"An awful looking dint, sir," the engineer shouted, as the captain climbed the ladder to the wheelhouse. "Without those thick steel bow plates we'd be going under."

"You go below," the captain bellowed to the engineer, "and see if she's sprung a leak along those plate seams."

Andrew crossed his fingers to bring them luck.

"She's not taking too much water," the engineer shouted up to him. "We'll have to use the pumps."

Andrew let out his breath in relief.

The early morning sun hung just above the ice, peering through a somber purple haze. Andrew looked up at the crow's nest fixed to the top of the stubby steel mast. He saw Mr. Smithers, the first mate, point, then cup his hands and shout down to the captain.

"The ice has opened up a bit, sir. I can see black water over near the river's mouth. The morning tide is starting to spread the pack ice."

"Do you see their small boat anywhere?" the captain hollered up to him.

Andrew watched the mate examine the coastline with his heavy binoculars, searching along the shore toward the river's mouth.

"No, sir," the mate answered. "I can't see a thing except ice and rocks . . . unless that straight stick standing in the river cove could be their mast. But it's probably just a dead tree. If it were the trader's boat, they would be picking their way out through the openings in the ice by now."

"Get ready, Mr. Smithers. I'm going to let her drift

in gently, right against that big flattop of ice. Then
you hurry and offload the cargo for this post. I'm not
going to get caught and held again by grinding ice in
this damned place like last year."

"Aye! You're right, sir. This is a dangerous spot. The
highest tide in the whole world is right over there in
Leaf Bay."

"Never mind quoting me the tide tables, Mr. Smithers. You get those ice hooks ready to make fast. Do
you hear me?" the captain shouted irritably.

"'Aye, I do, sir! I'll offload the cargo quick enough.
But what about their clerk, young Stewart, sir?" the
mate called down to the captain.

"The clerk? Their clerk? Well—he can damn well
get off this ship of mine and out onto that ice with his
trading company's cargo. He belongs to them and not
to me. He can wait for that little boat of theirs to come
and pick him up. Go ahead, Mr. Smithers, break out a
nice red signal flag and give it to the boy so that he
can wave for help. *Get Moving.* Do you hear me, Mr.
Smithers! I don't trust the ice or weather in Ungava
Bay. The engineer is calling me up the pipe. He tells
me . . . we're leaking . . . all along the bow plate
seams."

That thought made the first mate hop nimbly down
the iron-runged ladder from the crow's nest. Andrew
listened carefully to his words.

"Well sir, if the wind comes off the land that piece of
ice will drift far out of here to . . . God alone knows
where. A little flag won't help that clerk of theirs. He's
nothing but a boy. I think we ought to give him food
to eat."

"Food to eat?" the captain shouted. "He'll be on that

ice with tons of food. Let him stuff himself with the trader's victuals, not with mine. Just you unload that cargo, Mr. Smithers. I'll do the thinking while I am master of this ship! Where the devil is my morning cup of tea?" the captain shouted as he went inside the wheelhouse on the bridge and slammed the door.

The first mate, who was from Liverpool, hurried past Andrew on the deck.

"I swear some charter captains can be a mite too thrifty!" he whispered. "I guess you heard him talking about you. There is nothing I can do. You come along and help unload the cargo, lad." Mr. Smithers spoke cheerfully. "We will go on to the other fur posts and try to come into the Chimo River later, when this blasted ice clears out. You tell the trader we'll try hard to come back maybe next month and pick up his bales of fur.

"You put on all the thickest socks and winter underwear you have—mitts, hats, sweaters, too; everything you've got. And take along some matches. You might need a signal fire. It grows deadly cold out there on that ice at night."

"At night?" exclaimed Andrew. "You mean the captain's just going to dump me off with the cargo onto that piece of floating ice and sail away?"

"That's what he said, lad, and that is what he'll do! Last year, we got caught here for a fortnight and nearly lost our ship in this treacherous ice. The old skipper won't let that occur again. Not jolly well if he can help it!"

There were about twenty tons of cargo marked for Fort Chimo, and the crew lowered it carefully onto the ice in strong rope slings. Andrew stood beside the first mate and double checked the numbers on every single bale and box. Only then did he sign the slips declaring everything had been received.

The mate had no idea that Andrew was not quite sixteen. Almost no one would have guessed that, for he was tall, with a confident face and broad shoulders and a narrow-hipped way of walking that made him seem much older than his years. Andrew had brown curly hair, not long, not really short, and a strong straight nose, gray eyes and even teeth. There was something about his large hands and the set of his neck that made people believe he was strong and capable. Andrew could not see this in himself. He still felt shy and awkward and never looked at his own image when he passed a mirror. He tried hard not to trip over things. His mother had told him that he would soon get over that.

The four crew members who had been working down on the ice during the unloading climbed stiffly up the rope ladder and onto the steel deck. The last one aboard shuddered and said to Andrew, "I won't be envying you tonight."

Ralph, the clerk who had shared Andrew's cabin, solemnly shook hands with him and whispered, "If that captain tries to put me over the side at Kovik, I swear to you I'll quit this fur trading company I'm working for there and then. I'll resign and go back south! All this ice gives me the shivers!"

"Well, goodbye and good luck to you, laddie," said Mr. Smithers shaking Andrew's hand. "Have a pleasant summer. Here's your signal flag. Don't be afraid to use it. Now, over the side you go. We shall all hope to see you in a month or so, before it freezes up again—God willing. Don't worry, I'll ask the old man to let off a few blasts on the ship's horn to try and wake those landlubbers, if that's them sleeping in the river cove. We tried to radio them but there's too much static. Anyway they ought to keep a watch. They know it's the time of year that they should meet us here."

Andrew stood among the boxes on the ice and watched the black smoke rising from the freighter's single stack as the pressure in the boilers rose and her twin propellers churned the water into icy foam. Andrew could hear the pumps and see the huge dent in her steel-sheathed bow just at the water line. True to his word, the mate had the ship's horn give out three great blasts. Slowly the freighter worked back and forth until she was turned full stern to Andrew. As she eased north along the ice lead, Andrew waved his signal flag and saw Ralph, his cabin mate, wave back at him.

Andrew looked at his wristwatch. It was exactly 6:07 in the morning. To keep warm, he paced back and forth on his frozen island. It was almost the same size as the small ship that had left him there. The ice beneath his feet was perhaps ten feet thick.

About noon a light cold wind sprang up and Andrew shifted the bales and boxes to form a shelter for himself. He wedged the signal flag so it flew above his head and watched the windswept clouds spread out like mares' tails all across the southern sky. Then he climbed onto the tallest box and looked toward the river's mouth. He too could see the mast half a mile away—or was it a stripped tree standing needle-thin and motionless? It seemed his only hope. He had never known such loneliness in all his life.

Andrew tried to forget the cold and the moving ice. He tried to make his thoughts leap south across the frozen bay over the thousand endless miles of forests, lakes and rivers in Quebec. He tried to think of his mother and father, who would have long since left Montreal and returned south to their New England home. He wondered if New England was really his home too. He had lived with his family in many places. He had been born in Edinburgh, in Scotland, had first gone to school in Christ Church, New Zealand, then in San Francisco, and finally in Montreal in 1946. That's what it was to have a father who was an international banker.

"These days true Scots are only born in Scotland," Andrew's father had told him somewhat proudly. "From there the young must set forth to make their livelihood in every country round the world. They cannot stay home and earn their fortunes." That was what his father had done. He had left his homeland behind.

His father had added, "Most Canadians have always clung tight to their southern border. That's been a great mistake of theirs. The future of their country lies in the north. The Americans used to say, 'Go west, young man,' but today the message should be 'Go north!' That land up there is full of undiscovered treasure. But men must go there and sweat and freeze to find it!"

Well, thought Andrew, my dad would need an ice pick here to find any treasure. He wished his father could be with him now, searching for a fortune on a field of drifting ice!

As evening came the sky grew darker and the wind

moaned above his head. Shivering, Andrew again climbed up onto the highest box and searched the low black coastline. He shouted aloud with joy when he saw that the needle-thin mast in the cove had moved. But as he shaded his eyes against the wind, he realized that the mastlike stick had remained where it had been and that the ice on which he stood was moving northward into the huge expanses of Ungava Bay.

"Help me! Help meee!" Andrew shouted and waved his flag toward the sliver of the tree or mast, knowing full well that his voice would not be heard.

He went to the case marked Seaman's Pilot Biscuits and tried hard to pry or kick it open. But the wooden box was strapped with metal and was strongly nailed. His hunger knawed at him and the night cold seeped through his clothing. Andrew buried his face in his hood and curled up in the shelter of the boxes. He lost consciousness.

Andrew did not wake until he heard the ice creaking. He shuddered not just from the cold but from an eerie feeling that he was not alone. He sat up in horror when he saw a gnarled and bony hand creep around the corner of a box. Its fingers reached out to clutch his throat. Andrew screamed in terror, kicked out with his feet and flung up his arms to defend himself.

II

A Bad Joke

"NO NEED TO BE AFRAID OF ME, LADDIE," SAID A ROUGH voice from the semi-darkness. "I'm glad to see that you're alive and kicking."

Andrew leaned back against the boxes as he remembered where he was.

A broad-shouldered man appeared before him in a work-worn parka. He had on a moss green tam-o'-shanter hat and knee-high sealskin boots tied with bright woolen ribbons.

"Where did that blasted captain go?" the old man raged. "We've got a sick man here whom we were planning to send out aboard that ship. Where is it?"

"The captain was worried about the ice," said Andrew. "He just went off and left me out here with all the cargo. He was in a hurry to get his ship away."

"Well, it's not your fault, lad. It's only George not going that worries me. We've come to get you, my boy, and this costly cargo, which we intend to load aboard

11

our Peterhead boat. There's such a pile of goods this year," he said as he looked at them, "that you may have to perch atop our mast."

Andrew looked where the old man's finger pointed and saw a stubby white boat trimmed with green. The single-masted vessel was anchored fast to the ice on which they stood. A short, powerful man and a tall thin youth were already busy loading some of the lighter boxes and bales of cargo into the boat's hold. Another figure huddled on the deck with his hood pulled up, arms crossed and his hands hidden beneath his armpits, watching the others work.

"Come along with me," the old man said. "We'll be glad to have your help. This ice island of yours is moving in the wrong direction. Over there is land.

"Now you're going to meet our clerk, George. He slipped on the ice and strained his back. He can't pick up anything heavy and some mornings he can hardly get himself out of bed. He hasn't been a good clerk and he hasn't been happy here. Mr. McFee, the post factor, wanted to send him south not only because of his back, but because he'll never be one of us. Now George will have to wait here until that ship comes back again. Let me warn you about something," the old man whispered to Andrew. "Since George hurt his back, he has become more crotchety and bad-tempered. He's snappy and often mean with all of us. He can't help it. I guess he's in pain and now I don't know how long he'll have to wait before he leaves this place."

The snow squealed beneath their boots as they walked across the ice.

"What name did your family give you?" the old man asked him.

"Stewart, sir. Andrew Stewart."

"Well. That's a bonnie name ye have. I, myself, come from an isle of the Outer Hebrides. Long ago we hid a royal Stewart up there, yes we did, then sent him safely off to France."

When they reached the boat, the old Scot introduced Andrew. "Our new apprentice, Andrew Stewart."

Then he explained, "This is our clerk, George," pointing to the young man whose stark face was almost buried in his hood.

George shook hands carefully and stared coldly at Andrew.

"And this is Nakasuk," Dougal said, nodding his head toward a short stocky Eskimo who smiled broadly at Andrew and shook hands. "This lad here is Pashak. He speaks English very well. He's a Naskapi Indian boy I'd judge to be about your age. And then there's me. My name's Angus MacDougal, but most here just call me Dougal. I'm a boat-builder by trade, but here at Fort Chimo they only offer me the roughest sort of carpentry."

George, the clerk, did nothing to help them except mark each item as it came aboard. Andrew was surprised how quickly they loaded the twenty tons of bulky cargo onto the thirty-five-foot North Sea trawler.

"Jump aboard!" Dougal called to Andrew. "You can say goodbye now to your piece of frozen seawater. Hurry or we will never find a passage back to the river through this ice."

"Aw, don't let him worry you," said Pashak. "Nakasuk here will find the way. Eskimos are at their very best when piloting in heavy ice."

They watched old Dougal duck down into the aft

cabin and twist the heavy brass fly wheel once, twice, three times before it started the ancient engine. Nakasuk held the tiller in the square stern while he guided the boat first east then west, picking his way carefully through the loosening skeins of ice as the immense tide rose and turned and flooded back toward the river.

"There's the right way to go, see? Nakasuk found it!" said Pashak, proudly pointing forward.

Andrew saw that the ice had opened like an enormous jigsaw puzzle and left a cold blue pathway through its treacherous jaws.

"We're almost into the river's mouth. We're safe," Pashak called out to Andrew. "You ever been up north before?"

"No," said Andrew. "How far is it from here until we reach the trading post?"

"Oh, this is a big river," said Pashak. "We travel almost half a day from here to reach the post. This is my people's river, my home."

"*Uvungalo*," Nakasuk called to him.

"Oh, yes," said Pashak smiling. "Nakasuk says the Koksoak is his big river, too. Half-Naskapi, half-Inuit, I guess you'd call this river." He looked up at the morning sun.

"Come on," said Pashak. "Come down into the engine room where it's warm. You need a cup of Dougal's strong black tea."

As he drank his tea and ate a pilot biscuit, Andrew looked at Pashak. He was tall and lean, with a hawklike face burned dark brown by the glaring spring sun. He had large black eyes that moved as quick as any animal's. But when Pashak saw Andrew looking at him, he turned his head away shyly and even drew his sensitive, long-fingered hands up into his loose sleeves.

Warmed by the hot tea, Andrew began to nod. His eyes were closed when Pashak shook him and said, "Dangerous to sleep down here. Not enough air. Poison smells might kill you."

To let in some fresh air, Dougal opened up the hatch and the small round porthole. Pashak led Andrew forward to the foc'sle. "You sleep down there in the bunk," he said. "I got a caribou skin. It's soft. I'll sleep in the hold on top of the boxes."

When Andrew climbed down into the small foc'sle, he saw George, the clerk, lying stiff on his back, asleep.

Andrew woke at the sound of voices overhead and felt the bow of the Peterhead lightly touch against a dock.

Pashak shot open the small door above the foc'sle and said, "Androoo, you come up here—see your new home. You wake up George. Shake him carefully or you'll hurt his back."

Andrew touched George, who opened his eyes, then closed them tight as if in pain.

"We're here," Andrew said. "We're at Fort Chimo." He stuck his head up out of the foc'sle, blinking his eyes in the afternoon light. He could see that they were already tied to a long, narrow, wooden wharf that led to a white building with a bright red roof.

"That's the warehouse where we're going to store this cargo before it rains and rusts the rifles and hardens all the flour. Up there, that's the factor's house," said Pashak. "That's where you are going to eat and sleep.

Get ready. See that tall man? That's the factor, Alistair McFee. Here he comes!" Pashak added in a whisper. "You better get out there and shake hands nice and say hello."

When the factor reached the dock, he was waving wildly with a large blue handkerchief.

"Should I wave back at him?" Andrew asked Pashak.

"Oh no." Pashak laughed. "He's not waving at you. He's fighting off the mosquitoes. We got quite a few around here in summer."

"I can see that!" Andrew replied and he, too, started slapping at the mosquitoes that came in singing hordes around him.

"So, you must be the new apprentice clerk. What's your name?" the factor asked.

"Andrew Stewart, sir," said Andrew.

"Well, that's a solid sort of name." Alistair McFee laughed. "Did you send George off safely on the ship?" the factor called to Dougal.

"Unfortunately, no," Dougal answered.

"Androo just woke him, sir," Pashak said quickly. "He's coming up right away."

"What's that?" said Alistair McFee. "Do you mean to say George didn't get out on the ship?"

"No, sir," said Andrew. "The ship slung the cargo and me out on the ice and left before your boat arrived."

The factor shouted, "George, I'm really sorry. You should have been picked up by that charter ship and transferred to a government ice breaker with a doctor aboard to go south with them."

"That's the kind of rotten luck I have," said George. "I'll go when I can," he grumbled. "They'll probably come back for the fur."

As George came slowly up the ladder, he scowled at Andrew again.

Looking ashore, Andrew saw a crowd of people had gathered on the river bank. About half of them stood on the north side of the wharf. They were mostly short with broad brown faces. The men wore white canvas parkas trimmed with red, blue, or green braid, and all of them wore soft knee-length sealskin boots. Some of the women had on long-tailed parkas, and many carried babies who peeked out of their hoods.

On the south side of the wharf sat Pashak's people, the Naskapi. They were truly dark, their faces burned mahogany brown from the glaring sun of spring. When they spoke occasionally their bright teeth flashed, but Andrew could hear no sound from this distance. Their clothes were somber brown and seemed to blend in with the river bank. For long moments it seemed to Andrew that they did not move or speak at all. They sat as still as watchful animals observing every movement, yet making none themselves. Even the smallest children seemed to wait, motionless, like large-eyed dolls.

"We go to work now," Pashak said. "Tomorrow, Androoo, I take you to my father's tent. You meet my whole family."

The separate lines of Eskimos and Indians moved toward them on the narrow dock and began to fling large sacks of flour across their backs. They also hauled out of the boat's hold square chests of tea and ammunition, heavy rifle boxes and bales of blankets, coils of rope and kegs of nails, and a hundred other items for the whole year's trading. It was long past midnight, but still light, before they had every article stored safely in the warehouse.

"What are those lights across the river?" Andrew asked when they were done.

"Oh, those are lights from the opposition trader's house," Pashak answered. "We try to get all the fur. They try to get all the fur. They're a French fur-trading company. I'll tell you more about them later."

When Andrew went up to their company house, the trader showed him a small room off the main one. "This will be yours, Andrew Stewart. It's small but easy to keep tidy. When I first came into the country as an apprentice clerk, we used to have to curl up in a blanket behind the stove in winter and sleep down in the un-heated warehouse during summer. It's a lot better now." Back in the main room, he said, "Sit yourself down there on the bench next to George and we'll have our late-night supper."

The factor carved a roast of caribou that tasted like the finest beef. When they were finished, Andrew looked around him. The trader's house was big, but with low ceilings to hold down the heat. There were small windows, double-paned against the winter's cold.

There was nothing fancy about that house, for only men ate there and slept in it. There were no curtains on the windows, and no carpets on the floors. There was one long table, almost as thick and strong as a butcher's block, with a long bench on either side. The scattering of heavy tin plates and dented cups had been laid out by a silent Eskimo woman who moved through the lamplight of the large, cold room as quietly as a cat in her soft-soled sealskin boots.

Next morning, when they sat down to breakfast, Mr. McFee said to Andrew, "There are no tricks at all to honest trading. All you have to know is what a fur pelt is worth and what the trading goods are worth. Then lay the brass trading tokens on the counter and begin."

"What are the brass tokens used for?" asked Andrew.

"They represent amounts of money, but they never leave our store. A hunter may bring in a bundle of fur worth sixty-five dollars. You would lay five ten-dollar brass tokens on the counter and fifteen one-dollar tokens. When he buys two blankets, for example, each worth fifteen dollars, you take away three big tokens. When his wife wants spools of thread and needles worth two dollars, you take away two small tokens. In this way, the hunter knows at all times during the trading how much he has spent and how much he has left to spend. For a person who has not studied arithmetic, it is a good system.

"Once you understand the price of our trade goods and the current value of their fur, all you have to do is be watchful and polite and do your trading fairly. Dougal will teach you to grade fur and judge the value of the women's baskets.

"I wish I could help you get started this morning, but I have accounts to do up here, and Dougal must repair the fur shed. George has had enough experience as a clerk. He will help you make a start."

When they reached the store, George handed Andrew the broom, then leaned stiffly against the counter, watching him sweep the floor.

"Here they come," he said to Andrew in a few minutes, and he pointed down the path where a dozen young Naskapi hunters were coming toward them. "You go ahead and trade this first lot," George told Andrew.

"What will I say to them?"

"Well." George scowled. "That first man probably has otter skins inside his pack and I've heard that he and his hunting companion want to trade them for a rifle. The first thing you do is call in Pashak. He'll interpret for you. All you have to remember is that an otter skin is worth ten dollars and the rifle they want is worth one hundred dollars. It takes about ten prime otter skins to buy one rifle. All you have to do is lay out ten big tokens on the counter.

George was right. The first young hunter did have otter. He flung them on the floor in front of the counter, then carefully examined the rifle that Andrew handed him. He asked how many skins they wanted for a trade.

Pashak asked Andrew who held up all his fingers and said, "Ten." He started to lay the brass tokens on the counter.

"Ten otter skins?" asked Pashak. "That's too much! You must be making a mistake."

Andrew looked at George and said, "Is ten right?"

George just scowled again at Andrew and did not answer.

Andrew turned to Pashak and said, "Yes, ten skins for this rifle."

Pashak frowned and shook his head but told the hunters ten, exactly as Andrew had indicated.

The young hunter snatched back all his otter skins, stuffing them angrily into his sack. He talked with the others in an excited, high-pitched voice, then pointed at the French trader's store across the river. All together the hunters rushed forward. Pashak shouted a warning, but it was too late. Andrew felt a dozen strong hands reach out and grab him and drag him violently across the counter.

III

Pashak's People

ANDREW STRUGGLED HARD BUT HIS FEET NEVER EVEN touched the floor. The door of the trading post was kicked open and he saw moccasined feet running and the ground moving beneath him as he was rushed down to the landing and out the long wharf.

"Liar!" the young hunters shouted in Naskapi, and with one mighty thrust they flung him forward.

Andrew felt all hands release him as he arched outward from the end of the dock doing a half-somersault in the air before he struck the icy waters of the Koksoak River. His weight carried him deep into the steel blue water. Desperately he stroked toward the surface, his lungs bursting for air. Every nerve in his body seemed to wither in the stabbing cold. He could feel himself being swept away from the wharf by the powerful river current.

The young hunters who had grabbed him and flung

him into the river again shouted, "Liar!" and indignantly turned their backs on him and walked away.

Andrew felt the leaden weight of his water-filled rubber boots dragging him down. Drawing a deep breath, he ducked his head beneath the surface and struggled to pull off first his right boot then his left. When this was done he swam as hard as he could toward the shore. But the river current was too strong. Panic began to rise in him.

"Androoo! Androoo!"

He looked up and saw Pashak running along the river bank, closely followed by Dougal.

"Stroke hard for shore, laddie!" the old man called to him. "Stroke harder, harder!"

Andrew might never have touched the land again if it had not been for the long, thin tent pole that Pashak held out to him. Andrew caught it and was dragged to safety.

"You're shivering like a dog, poor lad. You take off that soaking coat of yours and put this parka of mine around your shoulders." Dougal held it out to him. "It's no wonder you're cold after bathing in that freezing river. Let me look at you, Andrew. Are you all right? Speak to me, and try to stop your teeth from chattering. Icy water does strange things to people. Shocks them. Stops their hearts sometimes. I guess you'll survive if you trot a bit to warm yourself. Pashak will follow you to see that you don't fall down. Go up to the house quick now and change every stitch of your clothing," Dougal ordered. "Stand by the stove a bit. I'm sorry that George told you the wrong thing to tell those wild young hunters. I don't blame you if you're angry,"

Dougal added. "Pashak says that because you were told something wrong by George you did tell them a lie, and that's why they flung you in the river. *Six* prime otter skins buy one good rifle. They are worth more than George told you."

"That's so," said Pashak. "It was George's fault, not yours. He didn't used to make mistakes like that. It's because he's given up. He knows he's going away and he may be jealous that you are staying."

Andrew hobbled over the stones on the bank in his bare feet, saying, "It's my rubber boots I mind about most. They were brand new ones and now I'll have to work at least a week to earn enough for another pair. Besides that, I hate to have the hunters think I told a lie."

Pashak laughed. "You forget about the boots. My grandmother will make you a pair of moccasins. Everyone says she's the best sewer among all the *Nenenat*," he said proudly, using the Naskapis' word for themselves, meaning "the true people." "My grandmother will be glad to make you a pair like mine. They are a lot more comfortable than those hard boots you lost. My uncle once bought me a pair of hard store boots. I could barely walk in them. I threw them in the river just like you."

Andrew and Pashak had reached the young Naskapi hunters who had thrown Andrew in the river and had watched his rescue. Pashak stopped and said to them, "This is my friend, Androoo. He didn't mean to lie to you. Someone told him the wrong way to trade. You want to throw him in the river again, two of you come and try to throw the two of us in. Maybe we give *you* the swim next time!"

As they turned and walked away Pashak said to Andrew, "Now we get you some other clothes."

When Andrew had put on dry clothes and a pair of borrowed boots and had warmed up, they went back to the store. George was still leaning against the trading counter half-asleep.

"How many otter does a hunter pay for a thirty-thirty rifle?" Andrew asked him.

"Six," said George, "maybe seven if the skins are small."

"You told me ten," Andrew answered.

"I only said that as a joke," said George. "I just wanted to see what the Naskapi hunters would do to you."

"Well, now you know," said Andrew. "I hate telling lies to anyone. Don't ever tell me something wrong again," he warned George, who didn't bother to answer him.

When Pashak took Andrew to his family's tent, Andrew was surprised to see that there were more than a dozen wigwams. Each was made of a circular arrangement of poles covered with weathered gray canvas and old caribou skins with the hair scraped off them. Like the Naskapi themselves, these wigwams were difficult to see. They seemed to hide in the shapes of the rocky hills and stunted trees around them.

Women and children stood stock-still near outdoor fires and watched as Andrew trailed behind Pashak into the camp. Pashak ducked into the entrance to a large tent and Andrew followed him.

Inside there was so much smoke that Andrew's eyes stung and at first he could see nothing.

"You sit down on the floor like me," said Pashak. "Smoke not so bad down here, no mosquitoes either. That's my father over there, and that's my grandfather, and over there, taking care of the fire, that's my mother, and behind her on the mattress, that's my grandmother. She's the one who's cleaning that caribou skin. She's going to make the moccasins for you. You hold up your feet. She measure you."

Andrew did as he was told and the grandmother held a string against his boot sole.

Pashak laughed. "My grandmother says she never saw such big feet on a boy!"

Pashak's mother fished around inside the blackened meat pot hanging upon the fire in the center of the tent and found Andrew and her son two delicious pieces of boiled caribou.

"Oh, I can't forget to show you my new young sister," Pashak said.

Andrew watched as Pashak's mother proudly took a smiling baby girl out of a moss-filled bag that hung down by a long line from the high poles that held up the wigwam.

"My grandmother gives out the names in this family. She calls my sister Snowbird. Do you like that name?"

"Yes, I do," said Andrew. Then he started to cough from the smoke.

"You lie down flat. My mother fix the flap so wind don't blow the smoke down here. White men and mosquitoes, they hate smoke! We *Nenenat*, we don't mind the smoke too much. All we care is that the tent stay warm in winter. We laugh a lot and have good times in this wigwam, hear lots of stories from my grandmother and lovely singing from my grandfather. I like a tent," said Pashak. "It's easy to move anywhere you want. I can't get used to white man's houses. They're too big, with bright lights and frosty windows, doors that slam, floors that go creak, creak, creak!"

Andrew lay on the ground supporting himself on one elbow so that his head was below the smoke caused by the open fire. As he ate the caribou meat and listened to the family laughing and talking in their soft musical voices, he had the feeling that he had been inside this wigwam before, that this family, who were around him sharing their home and food with him, were somehow like his own true family.

Pashak's mother handed Andrew a red wool blanket. "She says you look tired," Pashak said. "You're welcome to stay here and sleep with us." And Andrew did.

Next morning Alistair McFee came to the store. "What's this I hear about Andrew getting thrown in the river for trying to cheat the young Naskapi hunters?"

"It wasn't my fault," said George. "I meant it as a kind of joke," he muttered. "I didn't think they'd throw this new boy in the river."

"I believe it's the pain in your back that causes you to do such thoughtless things to other people," said the factor. "I'm truly sorry that the charter ship was not able to take you out for medical care. The Eskimos say the ice is going, and I expect the ship will come back on its way south. You will go then. Dougal, you're a man of much experience. What would you do about all of this?" the factor asked him.

"Well," said old Dougal, "the harm's been done. Andrew's been flung into the river as have many other clerks before him. Anyone could tell that Andrew didn't want to lie to those young Naskapi hunters. He wishes to be friends with them. When George goes, I believe things will right themselves."

"George," the factor said, "we have a real problem with you, and I have got to find a way to solve it. I want you to do only the lightest kind of work here. Keep the books and rest whenever your back hurts. But don't make any more cruel jokes that hurt others or this company's reputation. Andrew and Pashak will do the heavier work. Do you understand me?"

"Yes," George answered, but he glared at Andrew as though the fault lay with him.

"Andrew, you try to learn everything you can about this country and Indian ways," the factor said. "Later on, if you prove strong enough and wise enough, I'll have a job for you that will be very difficult to do."

IV

Fort Chimo

THE LATE WEEKS OF JULY AND THE EARLY PART OF AUGUST
seemed to fly away for Andrew, so busy was he learning everything he could about the fur trade. Old Dougal showed him how to grade each fur pelt, how to shake it out so that the long guard hairs stood up and he could judge the denseness of the soft, rich undercoat. Andrew did almost twice as much work as he would have done if George's back had not been sprained. He found that he liked Fort Chimo and both the Indians and Eskimos who traded there.

One morning toward the end of August, Andrew saw the factor standing in the doorway, searching the far reaches of the river with his binoculars. He heard him mumbling.

"He should be back here by now! What's keeping that man so long?"

"Who are you looking for?" asked Andrew.

"That ship's captain who dropped you off on the ice.

He knows he's got to come back here after dropping cargo at the other ports. He still has to pick up our fur bales and poor George as well. With the main ice gone, I cannot imagine what he's waiting for."

"Will the captain bring the ship into the river?" Andrew asked.

"Why not?" asked Alistair McFee. "There's almost no ice now, and that river's mouth is wide enough and deep enough to take the whole Royal Navy."

Three mornings later Pashak knocked on Andrew's window pane.

"Get up and see the ship! She's back again, anchored down near McKay's Island. Dougal's getting the boat ready. He says he's going down there with the factor and the fur. They're taking George out with them."

Andrew and Pashak hurried out along the wharf as the last fur bales were being loaded on the small boat's deck.

There was George, holding his kit bag, ready to go, eager to leave and see city lights and crowds of people once again. Andrew and Pashak held out their hands to say goodbye to him.

"I guess I shouldn't have told you the wrong thing to say to those young hunters," George mumbled.

"That's past and done," said Andrew. "I hope your back gets better."

"I guess I've failed here," said George. "I'm glad I'm going away."

"Goodbye," said Pashak.

Andrew helped George ease himself from the wharf onto the boat.

"You and Pashak stay and mind the store," the factor said.

Dougal started up the engine and the Peterhead chugged out toward the ship. They did not come back until the tide turned and the vessel the company had chartered had gone down the river.

When they returned, old Dougal said to Andrew, "Oh, the factor he was mad. You should have seen him. He got red in the face and shouted at that captain. Said he'd report him. Said he had no right to risk your life, setting you out on the ice that way with all the precious cargo that could have drifted out to sea.

"Well, let's forget about all that now," Dougal went on, "and be glad that George has gone and that all our fur is safely off to the auction house in southern Canada. Now we can settle down and have a lovely peaceful winter by ourselves."

"Andrew, how much do you know about a rifle?" the factor asked him the next day.

"Only that you aim at what you want to shoot and pull the trigger."

"Wrong, lad. You don't pull the trigger, you squeeze it very gently. Take this, and this," he said, handing Andrew the rifle and Pashak a box of cartridges. "You two go and practice."

Pashak led Andrew to his father's tent. He went inside and came out carrying a bow and a handful of arrows.

"What are you doing with that bow?" said Andrew. "The factor told us to practice with the rifle."

"First things first," said Pashak. He held up a thin,

carved piece of wood. "You know what this is?" Pashak
asked him.

"It looks like a deer," said Andrew.

"It's a caribou," said Pashak and he stood it up against
a mossy bank.

"Hit it in the middle," he said, handing the bow to
Andrew, who notched an arrow and took careful aim.
He missed by at least four feet.

"Here, I'll show you how," said Pashak, and he did.

By the end of the day Andrew could hit the wooden
target more than half the time.

"That's good," said Pashak, "and you'll improve with
practice. You learn fast. Tomorrow we'll try the rifle."

The target that Pashak brought with him next day
was much smaller and he placed it so that the bullets
would go into a heavy bank of earth.

"You've got to be very careful with a rifle," he said.
"One mistake and somebody could get killed. Kneel
down when you're going to shoot." Pashak demon-
strated. "Steady the rifle, like this—with your elbow
propped up on your knee. Crouching like that, the animals don't see so much of you."

When Andrew had fired seven of the twenty cartridges, Pashak stopped him. "Why not shoot the rest?"
Andrew asked.

"There's no need to do that," Pashak said. "You understand what you're doing now. And you hit the target with your last two shots. We save the other bullets,"
he added, putting them carefully into his hunting
pouch. "We may need them later."

One day at the end of August Pashak and Andrew,
who had learned to handle a canoe together, were pad-

dling north, practicing their skill and riding easily on the outgoing tide. They stopped when they came to a wide-rushing stream that flowed into the main river.

"You'll like this place," said Pashak as he steered to shore.

They pulled the canoe high, and because the mosquitoes were gone, they lay down on the sun-warmed rocks and fell asleep. When they awoke, a cool wind was blowing. The tide had turned and was flooding back into the river, forcing water up the stream until it almost covered the small waterfall.

"See them, see them?" Pashak whispered to Andrew, pointing at sleek salmon newly arrived in the tributary of the river.

The fish lay in schools, heads pointing upstream, flashing their silver sides in the ice cold, clear water.

"Oh, I wish we had fishing rods to catch them," Andrew said.

"We don't need rods," said Pashak. "Come and help me."

Andrew could see that hundreds of the big fish were lying inside a huge circle of stones set in the stream and now almost covered with water. There were only two narrow outlets.

"Wade in quietly," said Pashak. "You close that opening with those stones, and I'll close this one. When you start, move fast!"

Andrew saw several salmon slip out of the opening as he reached down. Wetting his arms to the elbows, he rolled three heavy stones to seal off one exit. Pashak did the same with the other. The big fish darted around in circles, searching for some escape.

"We've got them all!" Andrew shouted.

"No we haven't," Pashak said. "This is an Eskimo fish weir. Their grandfather's fathers built it very long ago. Eskimos don't mind if we take just one fish each, but no more. Hurry," he said. "When the tide rises full, this trap will overflow and all the fish will swim free again."

"How shall we catch even two of them?" said Andrew.

"I'll show you," Pashak answered.

He quickly cut two green sticks, one almost as long as he was, the other short. On the insides of both sticks he cut sharp notches, then with a piece of braided caribou sinew bound them tightly together at the top. He showed Andrew how the two green sticks sprang open when he pulled on them, then snapped closed like jaws with teeth.

Pashak waded into the water again and stood still, the sticks poised ready. Then suddenly he drove them downward, like a spear. He gave a mighty heave and flung a huge salmon, caught between the sticks, onto the bank near Andrew, who jumped forward, caught his fingers through its gills and dragged it away from the water.

"Now it's your turn," Pashak called, and wading out, resharpened the blunted teeth and handed his crude spear to Andrew.

"Missed!" called Andrew disappointed.

"Try again." Pashak laughed.

On the fourth thrust, Andrew saw the spear's jaws open over a salmon's back. He flung it straight at Pashak.

"Good." Pashak laughed again. "Keep on learning,

Androoo. When you can run on snowshoes, you'll become a true man, maybe."

"Do you think you two can manage an outpost at Ghost Lake?" the factor asked them a short time later. "It's a long, hard journey inland. I had planned that George would go, but now he's left and I guess it's up to you, Andrew, and Pashak, too. You're only an apprentice, Andrew, and you've been here only three months, not the two full years the company requires before you go out on your own. It's a big responsibility," said the factor. "You have your own selves to care for and others, if they need your help. And you have the honor of this company to uphold. This fort was built here by the company more than a hundred years ago. You must be as strong as all of those who have gone before you."

"We shall try our best," said Andrew. "Pashak's been showing me how to live off the land and read the weather signs. And Dougal's shown me how to grade the different furs."

"We'll be glad to go inland together," Pashak said. "Androoo, he learns things very fast."

"Well then," said Mr. McFee, "you two start to get everything ready for a long, cold winter on your own. I'm sure Pashak's family will sew some caribou skin clothing for you, Andrew: warm inner socks and moccasins and heavy mitts. You can trade them fairly for everything they make for you."

Andrew found that he had more time now that the summer trading was over and the Eskimos had loaded their long boats and their kayaks and had departed north. Many of the Naskapi families had also slipped away like shadows, traveling by canoe along one of the three mighty rivers that led south across the vast inland wilderness of the Ungava.

Pashak often asked Andrew to visit with his family and it was there that he first heard the *Nenenat* stories of the dwarflike creatures that live in stone caves beneath the earth and of the monsters that were said to dwell beneath the waters of the rivers and the lakes. Andrew came to know and like everyone in Pashak's family. Often in the evenings when they lay beside the fire, he felt as though he were at home, and he tried to imagine his own father lying comfortably on the floor talking to him, laughing with him in the same way that Pashak's father talked to him.

Andrew trembled when he thought of leaving all this and going out into the wilderness to live a completely different life.

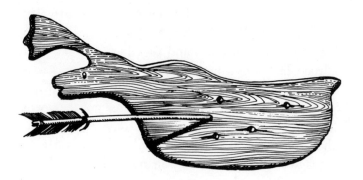

V

Night Wolves

ON THE LAST NIGHT IN OCTOBER, WHEN THE AUTUMN MOON was full, the weather turned deadly cold. A light frisk of dry snow came and covered the river banks and spread white mantles over the twisted branches of the dwarf spruce trees. The river had silver edges of ice that grew slowly outward trying to reach each other across the moon-streaked path of blackened water.

"It's coming," Pashak said to Andrew. "I can smell winter coming to us. I can hear it laughing, singing high above us in the air. Winter is my favorite time in all the year!"

Andrew sniffed the night wind and listened. He watched the stars flash in the sky like bright chips flung around the north star.

At dawn on November second, a huge wind came moaning out of the north and with it came heavy snow, burying the land and heaping white drifts against the wigwams of the true people. Three days later the blizzard died and after it a deadly chill crept all around them.

Andrew rose in the darkness of the night and hopped from one foot to the other on the freezing floor as he peered out of his frost-edged window. Only a narrow black path of water still remained in the very center of the ice-bound river. All the rest was frozen from both banks.

On the following night, the river closed, locked solidly, so that a heavy man could safely walk across it. Andrew could hear the ice moan and bang like distant rifle fire as it stretched and grew thick and strong.

In the morning Pashak came tapping on the window pane. "Androoo! Get up! My family sends a very good present to you."

Andrew pulled on his moccasins and all his heaviest clothes. The door hinges squealed with cold when he went outside.

Pashak held out a new pair of finely woven snowshoes. They were wide and round, of the beaver-tail type.

"They're yours," Pashak said. "My father carved the wooden frames, and my mother wove the webs. She sewed red tufts of wool on the tips of your snowshoes so you can easily tell them from all others."

Andrew had never seen a pair so delicately made. The caribou webbing of each snowshoe was like a tennis racket, but double woven and far more finely strung.

"You're lucky you got moccasins because you can't wear boots with light snowshoes like these."

Pashak held one foot up to show Andrew how to lash the binding. Andrew could scarcely wait to try them.

"Now you follow me," said Pashak, and he started off at a bounding pace.

Andrew tried to follow him, but tripped and fell head over heels in the soft deep snow.

"Not so easy as it looks," called Pashak. "But soon you'll learn. Roll your hips when you walk and hold your legs stiff and swing them out. Way out like this! That way you won't fall on your face."

"Phew!" Andrew laughed. "It's hard work to keep your legs so far apart."

Because people had gone and there was no trading today, they practiced together until the autumn sky grew dark. Andrew was glad to take his snowshoes off and eat his evening meal and tumble into bed. In the morning his leg muscles were so stiff he could scarcely rise. He walked into the breakfast table moving as awkwardly as a tin woodsman.

The factor laughed at him. "I remember my first time on snowshoes. It's worse than the first day on a horse. Keep practicing with Pashak and you'll get the hang of it."

Every day, Andrew spent hours on his snowshoes, learning the rhythm and the tricks of walking in this strange way. With Pashak's help, he even learned to move with some speed. Then one morning Pashak appeared again at Andrew's window. He had a huge pack on his back, and another one of equal size lay resting on the snow.

"Come on, Androoo, you got to learn to carry a little something on your back."

"A little something?" Andrew cried, when Pashak heaved the great weight onto his back. "What have you got in this pack? Stones?"

"That's right! Round river stones wrapped in old caribou skin. That's to make it easy for you. Here, put this tump line across your forehead and lean forward. That way your head and neck help do the carrying."

Andrew started off awkwardly, waddling like a duck. The huge weight of the pack, which extended from the top of his head to the top of his legs and which was wider than his body, pressed him deep into the new powder snow.

"I couldn't go far with a load like this," he gasped.

"Oh yes, you could," said Pashak. "You've got to learn. Our packmen often carry a load of meat three times that weight and they go all day long and sometimes half the night."

"On snowshoes?" Andrew was amazed.

"Sure!" Pashak answered. "How else you going to travel in deep snow except with snowshoes? In the winter forest snow comes up to here." He held his hand chest high. "You got no snowshoes, then you might as well sit down and wait to die."

"Do we have to carry everything inland on our backs?" said Andrew.

"Oh, no," said Pashak. "We're going to take some dogs and two toboggans with us. See them standing upright in the snow by those trees?"

They went over to inspect them. The toboggans were very narrow and thin-shaved, with delicate high-curving prows. Pashak took a candle from his pack, and holding it flat, rubbed it all along the bottom surface of the shortest toboggan. Then he placed his moccasined foot on it and gave a slight push. It went skidding far across the snow.

"See how the wax helps it? We'll ask the factor to give us half a box of candles. Make our toboggans go like two young otters playing on a slide."

"I can hardly move another step," said Andrew, when they came to Pashak's father's tent.

He sat down on a stone to ease his pack off.

"No wonder you have a hard time with the snowshoes and the pack," said Pashak. "Your heavy clothes are all wrong and your pack straps don't yet fit you right."

When they went inside the tent, Andrew was glad to lie down, stretched out beneath the smoke.

"My mother says you should try these leggings on."

Pashak's mother handed Andrew a loose-fitting pair of caribou leggings. He took off his pants and put them on.

"Thank you," he said. "They make my legs feel free but without those thick wool pants I think I'll freeze to death."

"Oh no, you won't," said Pashak. "Packing and snowshoeing keep you warm. Only around the face and in between the legs you got to be very careful of freezing. "Here," he said. "My grandfather gives you this nice bushy fox tail. He says you put it underneath your leggings between your legs. You never freeze. And that way your legs are free to move quick as the wind."

"What's that your grandfather's doing?" asked Andrew. "Is he painting something?"

"Sure, he's painting a new coat for you. See how he does it."

Andrew watched as the old man took up a carved

piece of caribou antler and pressed it into some soft red ocher paint that he had mixed. Then he carefully pressed the antler onto the caribou skin coat, and when he pulled back his hand, it left a double-curved image. He did it again and again, forming a delicate design along the sleeves and coattails. The grandfather next picked up a short, curved willow stick and dipped it into ground black charcoal from the fire that had been mixed in a small wooden dish with the oil of fish eggs. Using it like a pen, he drew long graceful lines between the stamped patterns.

"My father gave me some white ermine skins to trade for this belt for you." Pashak handed Andrew a wide belt. "Don't you tell Mr. McFee, but I sneaked across the river after dark and bought it from the French trader. They call a belt like this a *centure flashé*. Look how beautiful it is with those lightning marks in every color. It's woven tight out of the finest wool. Makes you look like a big-chested man of the woods, and also it keeps your back and belly warm."

"Oh and I almost forgot this," Pashak added. "My grandmother made you a lovely hat. It hangs down warm, almost like an Eskimo parka hood, but it's not sewn to your coat. There are some blue teal duck feathers tied so they stick out of the point. My grandmother says that gives you very good luck with the weather. Put it on your head.

"See! That hat is starting to be good luck for you already." Pashak laughed in delight. "You listen and you'll hear that wind dying all around us. My grandfather says it might be a good day for traveling tomorrow. Cold makes the snow just hard enough for toboggans to run fast out on the river. Look, my mother and my grandmother must want more tea and flour. They made us each six more pairs of moccasins. They say we wear them out and might not have a woman to sew for us.

"Come on, Androoo, put on your new clothes and we'll go and ask the factor when we can pack up and leave. When I was over there across the river, I heard that the French trader has a man out watching our trading post with a telescope all day every day, to see when and where we're going to go to build our new outpost. Soon as the French know that, they'll send someone to follow us to build their outpost next to ours—to split the trade. Their women over there, they listen all night to hear our dog bells. The trader on the other side believes we'll sneak out at night without them seeing us."

They found Alistair McFee at the store with Nakasuk and Dougal.

"Andrew Stewart, I'd never have guessed you were a Scot in those clothes," the factor said. "I thought you were pure Naskapi."

When they started talking about the opposition trader across the river, Dougal said to the factor, "I have an old poacher's idea. Why not send Nakasuk here packing north along the river with another Eskimo man and two toboggans with heavy-looking loads and all the dog bells ringing out like Christmas. When that other trader sees that, he might well make the mistake of sending his men racing up north after Nakasuk while our two smart lads run south with no one knowing."

"It's an idea worth trying," said the factor. "I'd like to outfox that wily trader over there. Hurry, Nakasuk!

You're leaving here tonight before it's dark. You stay away for at least four days, and if you're followed, try to lead them in a big wide circle. Oshaweetok will go with you."

"Andrew and Pashak, you and the packmen must start out quietly later tonight. Take the bells off the dog harnesses and don't let the women show a light."

"We'll slip out of here as silent as a school of salmon," Pashak said. "We'll stay behind the trees and won't go onto the ice until we're far beyond the river bend."

"That's it," the factor said. "I wish good luck to both of you. And because you're going to be away this whole long winter, I've a present for you." He went into the house and rolled out a sturdy wooden barrel of salt pork. "You'll be glad of that for a Christmas feast. Oh, and one thing more. Here's a rifle for you and a box of fifty shells. One gun's enough between you two. No need to carry more."

"Thank you, sir," said Andrew.

When the factor left, Pashak asked old Dougal if he had a wood drill. With it, Pashak bored a hole in the salt pork barrel, rolled it on its side and drained out all the liquid brine.

"Why are you doing that?" Andrew asked him.

"You think we're going to break our packmen's backs hauling salt water two hundred miles inland?"

Everybody was in a hurry to load the toboggans and send Nakasuk off. The evening sky turned flaming orange as he set out, with dog bells jangling, and headed north along the frozen river. Oshaweetok broke trail for them. He carried an enormous pack and tested the snow-covered ice with his long straight staff.

❉   ❉   ❉

"It worked. It worked," old Dougal crowed in delight. "We saw the French drivers leaving just at dark to follow Nakasuk and Oshaweetok deep into Eskimo country."

"You lads can go now," said Alister McFee. "Good traveling and good luck. We'll see you in the spring."

Just before midnight, when the moon hid its face behind a bank of clouds, Andrew knelt beside one of the loaded toboggans and bound on his snowshoes. Half a dozen strong Naskapi hunters bent and shouldered their enormous backpacks. Pashak helped Andrew into his. Excitement seemed to crowd around them.

"We two should start now before the others," Pashak whispered. "That way we get ahead and try to stay ahead. If you're at the end of the line, you'll fall far behind the others. Remember to swing your legs wide and easy," said Pashak. "I'll break trail for you. Stay close behind me. This first day will be the hardest."

They did not go down onto the river until they were well around its bend, far beyond the sight of the French trading post on the opposite side. The deep snow on the land was difficult and Andrew was gasping like a distance runner at the finish line by the time they beat their way down onto the soft snow covering the frozen river and commenced their long journey. Andrew had hoped that they would rest there, but the packmen were gaining on them fast. Andrew's heavy pack bit into his shoulders, but he remembered what Pashak had said—the first day will be the hardest, the hardest, the hardest!

He could hear the soft *swish, swish, swish* of snowshoes as the headman, carrying a tremendous pack, drew even with him and then passed him without a word or glance. Not long after that the second and third of the packmen passed him, then both teams of panting dogs, their drivers, and the heavily loaded toboggans moved around him. He would have given anything to flop down and lie flat, resting on the last toboggan, but no one offered help and his sense of pride kept him from asking for any.

Pashak, who had been keeping a steady pace in front of Andrew, said, "Why don't you let me carry the gun? It bumps against your leg and slows you down."

Andrew gratefully unslung the rifle from his shoulder and handed it to Pashak, who slowly started to increase the length of his stride and draw ahead. Andrew tried desperately to keep up with him. His shin muscles throbbed like two enormous toothaches and his backpack pressed down on him like a ton of lead. He tried but could not drive himself to keep pace with the lean and steady-striding Pashak.

The luminous hands on Andrew's watch said three in the morning. He forced himself along the frozen river. Ahead, he saw the Naskapi packmen moving together in single file. Their backpacks rippled up and down like a dark caterpillar as they disappeared around the river bend. Pashak was right behind them. Andrew hurried on, afraid to be alone, afraid that the clouds, which had gathered in the west, would breed into a storm and wipe away the packmen's tracks, the only trail he had to follow.

At four o'clock in the morning the waning moon appeared, running like a pale ghost through the clouds. Andrew stopped when he heard an eerie howling somewhere along the river bank. He waited with every muscle trembling. Cold sweat trickled down his back. In terror he heard answering howls. Wolf after wolf along the river bank had set up a deadly chorus signaling to each other that one helpless human straggler was coming up the frozen river, all alone!

VI

The Winter Trail

Wolves will not attack a healthy man. Wolves do not run in packs, though sometimes a family of wolves may hunt together.

Andrew had read this in a book. Now he wanted desperately to believe every word. He kept saying them over and over in his mind.

The stinging night cold seared his nostrils as he hurried onward, following the beaten file of snowshoe tracks. He had not traveled more than a mile when the clouds opened and the moon shone down brightly, lighting up the frozen river. Off to his left he saw the dark forms of a dozen wolves racing across the snow. He cursed himself for letting Pashak take the rifle from him just when he might need it for protection. Silently he crouched, trying to make himself small as he watched the wolves race past him and disappear into the gloom.

Hours later, driven by his fear, Andrew staggered

into the dark camp that the Naskapi packers had built
at nightfall. He hung his snowshoes high in a tree and
peered at the luminous hands on his watch. They said
that it was almost morning. Andrew crawled into the
low canvas tent and lay down among the true men.
Every one of them was fast asleep. Earlier the Naskapi
had built a roaring fire but it had crumbled into dying
embers and most of its warmth was gone. The Naskapi
slept on thick spruce branches that they had spread
over the snow around the fire pit. Each man was
wrapped tightly in his woolen trade blanket. They
rested with their feet almost in the fire.

When Andrew awoke it was daylight. The tent that
had covered him was gone. Everyone was gone and the
fire was black and cold. The sky above his head was
heavy with fat gray clouds, like pillows filled with goose
down, that hung so low they seemed almost to touch
the river banks.

Andrew looked at his wristwatch. It had stopped.
That meant that he had lost white man's time. It would
be a long while before he found it again.

He leaped up, rolled his blanket tight and bound on
his snowshoes. On top of his pack he found a chunk of
dried fish between two big, square hardtack biscuits.
Andrew ate greedily, then bent to heave his pack onto
his shoulders. He noticed that it was smaller and
weighed much less than it had the day before. He was
surprised and ashamed and yet grateful to some packer
for his kindness. He hurried south along the deep-trod
line of snowshoe tracks, massaging his stiff thigh muscles, running awkwardly, his mouth still full of cold
fish and biscuit crumbs.

By noon it was snowing lightly like layer upon layer

of soft blowing curtains drifting south across the river.
By evening his whole world was full of swirling snow.
Andrew could no longer see the river banks. The snowshoe tracks he followed had grown fainter and fainter.
Just before dark they entirely disappeared, so he decided to move in close to one bank of the river and follow it until he reached their camp.

Then something happened that frightened Andrew
far more than the howling wolves. Before him in the
gloom he saw low trees on a point of land where the
river narrowed and split into two separate branches.
One led into the southeast and the other straight south.

Andrew took off his heavy pack and, kneeling, tried
to see or even feel beneath the snow some impression
of the Naskapi tracks. But he found nothing.

In a wild panic he hurried down the southeast river
branch. Then, feeling that he was wrong, he turned
and rushed back, to start down the southwest branch.
An icy wind was rising, driving the blinding snow
against his face.

"Wait, wait!" Andrew cried aloud to no one but himself. "Stop and think! There may be some sign. Pashak
would have known I'd be in trouble here."

He stared around but saw nothing in the darkness.
Then off to his left Andrew heard a faint tinkling sound
only a short distance along the southeast arm of the
river. He followed the sound until he reached a short,
black spruce tree. There tied in its branches at the
level of Andrew's head hung a tin cup and next to it a
metal spoon. The wind made them strike together.

Gratefully Andrew untied Pashak's signals and put
them in his pack, certain now that he was on the right
trail. He wondered at Pashak's cleverness, leaving him

a sign that would guide him even in the blackness of night.

At what he guessed to be about midnight, when the moon was high, the snow stopped falling and the night wind blew the whole sky clear. Andrew was staggering with fatigue and hunger and yet he dared not stop. He could scarcely believe that the backpackers and their toboggan dogs could be so far ahead of him.

At the first light of dawn he saw a red smudge in the snow beside the river bank. When he reached it, morning had come. It was the Naskapi camp, but they had already packed their tent and gone. The ashes of their fire were cold. The red smudge that Andrew had seen was an old trade blanket they had rigged by bending down two trees to form a small shelter. Underneath the tent-like blanket they had spread spruce branches.

Painfully Andrew removed his heavy pack and then his snowshoes, which he hung high in a tree. Not bothering to try and light the fire, he crawled into the shelter and gnawed some dried caribou pemmican that Pashak had left for him. He rolled himself into his blanket. Too tired to think of his loneliness or his fear of wolves, he fell sound asleep.

Andrew woke suddenly and looked at his watch, forgetting it had stopped. He heard a harsh scream as a strange bird came and perched on his blanket less than an arm's length from his face. The bird was almost as large as a crow. It was shaped like a blue jay except that it was gray in color.

"Hello," said Andrew, "what do you want?"

As if in answer to his question, the bold bird hopped onto the pemmican bag near Andrew's head and began picking at the rich yellow fat.

"You must be very hungry to have lost all fear of humans," said Andrew. "Go ahead and have some meat. I'm glad you woke me." He stretched his arms and felt his muscles.

"I'll tell you something, bird," said Andrew. "I'm not going to sleep again until I run down Pashak and his friends. I'm getting tired of living out here all alone. You're the first real person I've spoken to in two whole days and nights. Well, you're not a person . . . but . . ." The gray bird cackled and flew away.

Andrew jumped up, rolled the red blanket they had left him, slung it across his pack, and started out. He believed that his snowshoeing was improving, but still by late evening he had not caught sight of the packmen. As he shuffled his wide snowshoes along the frozen river he heard the wolves again. Their ominous howling drove the tiredness out of his legs and made his half-weight pack seem lighter. The river bed narrowed and against the night sky he could see the dwarf spruce trees that lined both banks.

He turned a bend in the river and, wonder of wonders, saw a soft orange glow ahead of him. It was firelight on the snow, on the bank of the river. He broke into a run, so excited was he to see this sign of human life. When he drew near, the toboggan dogs set up a savage barking and he saw the silhouette of a true man come and stand outside the low tent.

"Androoo, Androoo!" a voice called to him. "I'm glad to see you. I was beginning to worry about you."

"Oh, I'm all right," said Andrew as he sagged down onto the snow and eased his aching shoulders out of the packstraps.

Pashak helped him as he unlaced his snowshoes and hung them in a tree beyond the dog's teeth as all the others had done.

"You come inside and eat with us," said Pashak. "You must be tired and hungry."

"I'm not so tired today as yesterday," said Andrew. "I'm getting better at snowshoeing. Today, at last, I caught you!"

"I don't like to tell you this," said Pashak sadly, "but I ask the packmen to slow down a little. I told them please to build our night camp early. I wanted them to wait for you. The packmen don't like to wait for anyone. They say if they wait, you're never going to learn to be a snowshoe man. It's good for you, they say, to have to run to catch the *Nenenat*—the true men," Pashak said with pride.

There was a babble of words from the packmen, when Andrew stepped inside the tent.

"They say they're glad to see you, Androoo," Pashak translated. The "first man," the *wotshimao*, with a face scar, smiled and pointed at the oatmeal porridge pot and blackened tea kettle and at his mouth, and said to Andrew, "EAT!"

Using a carved wooden spoon, Andrew devoured every last bite of porridge and washed it down with hot black tea. He rolled up in his blanket, lying like the others with his feet toward the fire.

Pashak listened to the *wotshimao* talking, then translated his words for Andrew.

"He tells the others you're getting better on the snowshoes. He says you must keep up with everyone tomorrow. Don't you let the two toboggans out of sight."

"Tell him I won't," said Andrew, and as he fell asleep he heard the wolves again, howling far along the river. It's good to be lying here safe among true men again, he thought, and not out there by myself on that lonely river.

A foot nudging him in the back woke Andrew, and, looking up, he saw Pashak standing there fully dressed. The old canvas tent that had been over his head had disappeared again.

"We let you sleep a little, but now you hurry. Don't let us out of your sight. Hurry, Androoo. Hurry!"

Pashak ran off along the river, working hard to catch the packmen. Andrew watched his beaver tail snowshoes flinging dry powdered snow into the cold, clear air.

Andrew tied up his blanket and bound on his wide wool belt and snowshoes. Only then did he see that his pack was gone. Gone? He looked everywhere. It had simply disappeared. He thought, they took away the gun, then half of my pack the second day, and now on the fourth day they've taken the rest of the pack. I'll keep up to them today, he vowed. They're loaded down and I am carrying nothing.

What he set out to do was far from easy. That day Andrew did not walk after the true men. He ran. Swinging his legs out painfully, trying to avoid tripping on his wide snowshoes, he marveled at how fast the Naskapi traveled along the snow-filled river. He did not catch the packmen until nightfall, when they started to make camp, but as he had promised Pashak, he had not once lost sight of them.

As they gobbled down dried caribou and drank hot tea, Pashak told him that the strong man who had taken

Andrew's pack on top of his own had said that he now believed Andrew might one day become a snowshoer.

"He's right," said Pashak. "We didn't slow down for you at all today. And many packmen here say they're surprised that you are with us tonight. They say if you keep trying, you might get to be a true man—just like us!"

Next morning, Pashak woke Andrew early and said, "Today you've got to do it right. Start out before us. Don't stop! Eat the pemmican and hardtack I give you. Eat it as you go. And keep ahead of us."

Andrew tried with all his might. He heaved on his own pack and started out ahead of everyone. By noon most of the packmen had almost caught him. By midafternoon three of the fastest packers had passed him. Andrew was so tired that he could have lain down and cried. But still he drove himself forward, feeling the packstrap biting into his shoulders so hard that his arms and hands were numb.

Pashak passed Andrew without saying a word. Then the "first man" drew even with him and, reaching out, silently took Andrew's pack without either of them missing a single stride. Andrew felt so light without the weight that he thought he might drift up into the air and float over the others.

Slowly he gained on Pashak and was about to pass him. He leaned in, without breaking his stride, and slipped the rifle from Pashak's shoulder.

"*Merci beaucoup*," said Pashak. "I learned that from the Frenchman across the river—it means thank you." No one said another word until dark, when they made camp and ate. They slept until dawn next morning.

"Only one more day and then we rest," said Pashak.

"We're coming to the caribou place. We need meat. We wait there one quarter or maybe half a moon. We can't go on without some food."

Andrew could see that the whole country was changing. Far north of them, near the coast of Ungava Bay, there had been almost no trees. Now he noticed that although he was still a thousand miles north of the St. Lawrence River the trees were becoming more numerous. They were mostly small spruce twisted by violent winds so that their branches grew just on the south sides of the trees. But now Andrew sometimes saw thin stands of white birch and some low ground willow and red alder growing on the river banks. The snow was deeper here and the river was sometimes crisscrossed by fox tracks. Once Pashak showed him the wide, soft, catlike prints of a lynx.

"The packmen say we should have seen lots of caribou tracks by now. But we have seen not one," Pashak said.

Long before they turned the far bend in the river, they could see two columns of thin white smoke rising straight into the cold blue evening sky.

"I hope that's the Mium-scum family." Pashak pointed at the smoke. "They usually camp here this time of year before the real cold comes."

"Before the real cold comes?" said Andrew. "I never dreamed that any place could be so bitter cold as this!"

"You just wait," said Pashak. "In the midwinter moon you'll know real cold. You'll hear the frozen sap explode inside the trees and fling the branches out from the trunks like broken spears and arrows. Then you'll see how the true men live in winter."

Pashak pointed up the river bank. "Androoo, you

keep your eyes wide open in this camp. You're going to see a very interesting family. And something else as well," he added, pointing at a tall, thin, bark house that stood by itself. "This is a magic house."

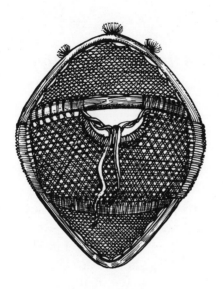

VII

Mium-scum's Camp

THE CARIBOU HAD NOT COME TO THE RIVER CROSSING. That could cause starvation.

The old man, Mium-scum, sat hunched inside the tattered tent, swaying slowly back and forth as though he were some huge, rough-feathered bird, his nose thrust forward like a great brown beak. He was worried. He tried to send his mind out searching for the caribou. He held a caribou antler in his left hand and ran his gnarled old fingers along its narrow grooves, channeled like small caribou paths across the tundra. Eyes squinting in the smoke, Mium-scum started humming magic words and tapped his fingernail against the antler, imitating the sound of caribou hooves clattering across stones. He cocked his head and listened for any secret sign or sound. He watched the fire for sparks that might rise up and drift toward the east or west, revealing some hidden route of the long-awaited caribou. His head nodded and his eyes closed

58

as he waited for a sacred vision to come to him. Nothing happened.

"Packmen coming on the river! Dogs pulling two toboggans!" Mium-scum heard the sharp-eyed children warning him through the smoke-stained tent walls. "They come in secret without dog bells. They are true men, our men, coming up the river. See how their snowshoe trail curves in toward our camp."

Osken, who had been sitting watching his father, rose and stepped silently toward the entrance. But old Mium-scum heard his son and coughed and drew another caribou sleeping skin about his shoulders. Osken eased back the tent flap and ducked outside. He drew in his breath and felt the hairs inside his nostrils stiffen as the freezing autumn air sent shivers trickling down his spine.

Mium-scum's curiosity forced him outside also. He shaded his old eyes and stared along the snow-filled reaches of the River Koksoak.

"You say men are coming?" he asked in a voice as rough as gravel.

"Yes, yes, we see eight men and two toboggans," his youngest daughter, Atich, whispered to him. "They are almost hidden in the shadow of the river bank," she added, remembering his failing eyesight. "Osken says they are *washkanenken inno*, Chimo packmen. Osken's young wife, Wapen, told him they are journeying inland to build a trading house."

Wapen looked with pleasure at the old man's strong, high-cheekboned face. "My brother Pashak may be with them."

"Start some fish soup brewing so that they will get the smell of it." Mium-scum chuckled. "If they are true men they will run up the hill and feast with us. We will see what happens after that."

Wapen and Atich flung some broken tree limbs on the outdoor fire causing showers of sparks to soar up into the cold night air.

"They see the fire. They smell the fish. They are running now!" Wapen called out, trembling with excitement. "I see Pashak hurrying to us with the line of moving men!"

"Eight, nine, ten dogs," the children counted.

"Pulling heavy gifts on two toboggans," Atich exclaimed. "The strongest men are coming to our feast!"

"Bring out all the largest trout," Mium-scum shouted to his daughter. "Hurry, boil them in our biggest kettle. Packing men are always hungry!"

"Oh, we shall feed them well," his daughter answered as she went running to the nearly empty fish cache, laughing with excitement. "Look, you can see the new red trade blankets tied across their packs. See the enormous loads they carry."

As they toiled up the long slope of the river bank, Pashak said to Andrew, "My sister Wapen is married to Osken, who is Mium-scum's son. They live in this camp. Not much . . . talk . . . tonight," Pashak added wearily. "Everyone's too tired. We eat . . . we sleep . . . tomorrow night the singing and the feasting." He paused. "I don't see meat hanging in the trees. I think they must have had a visit from the owl."

"A visit from the owl?" Andrew did not understand.

"Yes." Pashak nodded. "First they must have built their camp down there on low ground. Then I think an owl flew near their tents—bringing them bad luck.

Mium-scum, the headman, he would have had to move up here on high ground. Windy here, poor place to camp, but no owls fly up here. Owls prefer low ground and don't like to share it. Look, you see how my sister Wapen and the other women hang men's coats and hats and leggings outside to show the owl that they are wealthy people, that their hunters have got a change of clothes."

It was dark by the time all the packmen and the two toboggans arrived in Mium-scum's camp. Andrew and Pashak beat the dry snow from their leggings, trying to look as fresh as though their six-day journey had just begun. Mium-scum greeted each traveler as he came in and watched with pleasure while they unhitched their dogs and sniffed the rich thick lake trout soup.

"This is my young sister, Wapen," Pashak said to Andrew. "Her name means star."

Wapen was beautiful and shy, with huge dark eyes and a wide smile that showed the evenness of her strong white teeth. She wept with pleasure when she saw her brother, for she was newly married and still homesick for her family.

Working all together they took down the camp's two smaller tents and added the larger tent of the travelers to the long ridge pole that they erected. Soon they had a truly great tent, long enough so that it needed five fires to heat it. Now more than thirty people would be sleeping in the feasting lodge. They believed that with so many hunters they would soon be given meat.

The women spread thick spruce boughs on the tent floor in such a clever way that they formed beautiful designs around the five fireplaces. As soon as the fires were lighted, they gave the inside of the long lodge a warm, flickering glow. To see such an enormous feasting house set the children laughing aloud with pleasure.

The packmen gave out small presents, then lit up two new pipes, jammed full of the trader's twist tobacco, and passed them round the lodge. The tobacco was so strong that it set most people coughing miserably, but they pretended pleasure.

"So," gasped Mium-scum, choking until he could speak again. "I see that you have blankets, beads, and strong tobacco. We must tell you that almost half of all our fish are gone. We have no caribou."

Pashak said to Andrew, "The packmen are too tired to care. Food will come."

Andrew, himself, was one of the very first to fall asleep. Pashak's sister, Wapen, had to wake him. She warned Andrew to roll warmly in his blankets, for the fires would die and in the morning the big tent would be bitter cold.

Bitter cold it was! Ice had formed solidly in all of Mium-scum's blackened pots and kettles. Andrew woke and stared up at the hoarfrost hanging from the low gray canvas ceiling. He burrowed deeper into the warmth of his pair of blankets. Had he not made the six-day snowshoe journey and arrived here with the true men? He moved his legs. They felt not as stiff and painful as before, and only in two places could he feel where the packstraps had burned his shoulders. I know how to do it now, he thought. I'll never be left behind again.

When the women were up, Andrew and Pashak dug out a sack of oatmeal porridge and a stone jug of molasses. After it was cooked, everyone in the camp ate an enormous breakfast washed down with tea. Pashak and Andrew went outside to try and gauge the weather and feed the last of the porridge to the hungry dogs.

"Things are bad here," Pashak said. "They gave us too many fish to eat last night and we cannot give too many feasts of our dried meat and porridge or we'll never reach Ghost Lake."

"The caribou come nowhere near us," Wapen's husband said.

"No one here can imagine why they have not come," Pashak translated for Andrew. "Unless it was the owl who . . ."

"Oh, but that's just foolish superstition," Andrew interrupted him.

"Don't say that!" Pashak whispered. "Mium-scum has sent for the shaman. He is the only one who can bring the caribou to us now. That is why they have built a *mistapeo*, a magic house."

"Listen," Pashak said. "Atich says she sees someone coming."

"*Kosabattom! Kosabattom!*" she gasped as she ran inside the tent.

"*Kosabattom* means shaman," Pashak told Andrew. "He is called Cut Cheek. Just seeing him made some people in this camp curl up with fright."

As Cut Cheek drew closer, they could see the wild designs and figures painted on his clothing and on the prow of his toboggan. Some of the young ones ran and hid behind their parents when Cut Cheek came shambling toward them through the black spruce trees. They could see his skinny helper too, pushing the toboggan.

"Cut Cheek is here," the children shrieked. "His magic

will turn your feet into owl's claws," they told each other. "He will cause dreadful worms to crawl in and out of your ears."

"We will give him presents so that he will not harm you!" their parents said.

"Be quiet," growled Mium-scum. "That magic man has ears as sharp as any female fox. He hears every single word you say. I sent for that magic man to come here and help us find the caribou. I did not ask him to grow bird beaks on the mouths of noisy children. Do you hear me?"

To welcome the shaman the thick broth left in the big trade kettle from the night before was quickly hung above the outdoor fire, sending up the rich odor of lake trout simmering.

When Cut Cheek saw the young hunters watching him approach, he pulled the toboggan harness off his chest and flung it on the snow. "Let others haul our burden," he shouted to his skinny helper. "I am tired!"

He snatched a skin bag from beneath his toboggan lashings and shuffled forward to the place where the snow had been flattened and turned gray around the women's outdoor fire. Swiftly he unlaced his snow-shoes. His helper hung them in a tree and kicked a dog that came too close to Cut Cheek. Together they marched inside the long lodge without a word or even a glance at the tall magic house that had been built for the shaman alone.

VIII

The Magic Man

WHILE ALL THE PEOPLE OF THE CAMP WATCHED, CUT Cheek and his helper wolfed down the trout soup. Carelessly the magic man spat trout bones into the fire.

"What has happened to the caribou?" Mium-scum asked him. "When will they come to us?"

Cut Cheek tossed aside his empty bowl and wiped his hand across his mouth. Sneeringly, he said, "You want me to fly to *Katipinimitaoch*, the big-antlered man, and beg him for you, hoping he will send his warm-haired children to you?"

"That is so," Mium-scum said, and he stared through the rising wood smoke at the magic man, who gazed back at him in silence.

Cut Cheek lay resting on one elbow, his cruel eyes glowing in the firelight as watchful as a hungry lynx.

"How shall the caribou come to us?" Mium-scum asked him.

Cut Cheek's eyes moved from face to face, leering slyly at each one of them. "I have not asked. I do not know," he answered.

"Then will you go and speak for us?" Mium-scum begged him humbly. "We are four families here, and our visitors as well. Must we spread apart, or dare we stay and live together?"

"*Katipinimitaoch,* the caribou man, knows the answer to your question." Cut Cheek nodded his head toward the eastern spirit mountains.

"Will you go into the magic house and ask him?" said Mium-scum again, and he laid a new pipe and two twists of tobacco before the shaman as a gift.

Cut Cheek scoffed, turned away his head and shook his bag of magic amulets. "That is not an easy journey to be undertaken for a cheap pipe and a few twists of trade tobacco."

"Take this as well," said Mium-scum, placing his best steel crooked knife before the shaman.

The magic man, whose shirt bore painted symbols of the moon and stars and animals, half man and beast, stared coldly at the packmen and at Andrew and Pashak and at Mium-scum's hunters.

"The journey that you demand of me is very dangerous. I must fly faster than death's raven, who will surely try to pluck my eyes out."

Mium-scum's son laid out a precious coil of snare wire, and one of the packmen placed a small sack of hard rock candy near the shaman. Wapen and Mium-scum's daughter both unpinned silver brooches and laid them near the fire.

Cut Cheek scooped up all the gifts. "I'll get the

other presents from you later. Quickly now, hang up the drum!" he shouted to the skinny boy. "Everyone be quiet. I will try to reach the horned man for you." Cut Cheek threw spice needles on the fire and evil-smelling mice skins. As the thick smoke rose and filled the lodge, he began his mournful singing, keeping a steady beating rhythm on the tambourine-shaped drum. The first sounds he made sounded like a raven's cry.

"Kak, kak, kaaak!
Raven, help me, help me.
Raven, make a sky trail for me.
Make a sacred path for me.
Raven, lead me to the mountains,
To the giant antlered man.
Tell him I am coming.
The kosabattom *man is coming*
To beg help for the true men.
Kak kak, Kak kak
Kak, kak, kaaan!

"Drape the gift blanket round me, boy," he cried out in a quavering high-pitched voice. "I feel dark wings fluttering."

Quickly his boy helper unfolded the skins and blankets that must be hung up in the lodge to shield the shaman from the others' sight.

Andrew felt his head jerking and his fingers twitching as he listened with the others to the hypnotic pounding of the drum.

Cut Cheek craned his neck and shrugged his shoulders like a bird. "I feel like flying. Flying! Flying! You get outside this tent," he bellowed at his helper.

"I am going now," the shaman shrieked, and suddenly the whole lodge began to tremble as though shaken by a violent windstorm. "Higher! Higher! I go higher!" Cut Cheek's voice became a scream.

Even to Andrew it seemed that the shaman's voice soared high above them. The women wailed in fright, the children screamed, and the hunters held their breath, clasped their hands over their ears and stared wide-eyed at one another. They waited—no one knew how long—until far off in the east they heard the magic man flying back. They heard the *kak-kak-kak* of a raven winging swiftly toward them through the night sky. Suddenly the tent stopped shaking.

Still gasping, the shaman's skinny helper ran inside the tent and tore down the leather skins hanging from the lodge pole. Everyone could see that the shaman had disappeared. They ran to the magic house, and inside they found Cut Cheek trembling like a dying man. His face was pale and bathed in sweat.

"Did you see him?" Mium-scum shouted at him. "Did you see *Katipinimitaoch*? Did you see the antlered man?"

"Yes, yes, I saw him," Cut Cheek answered as his helper poured warm tea into his mouth.

"What did he say to you? What did he say?"

"Your first man shall be the one to lead you." Cut Cheek pointed at Mium-scum. "All of you shall hunt out there together."

He waved his hand toward the west and resumed his magic singing, beating time against the bark walls of the tall round spirit house.

"Turning, churning,
Fright and panic.
See them breast deep
In the snow . . ."

"What do the words mean?" Andrew whispered to Pashak who translated. "I still don't understand," said Andrew.

"I think he means that when the caribou do come, we should run them into a place where there is soft deep snow. Now he's saying that we should spear them without frightening others with the noise of guns. You notice," said Pashak, "that he does not use our word *atich,* meaning caribou."

When Cut Cheek's song had ended, and he was fanning the fire with a red hawk's tail, Andrew boldly asked him, "What does *Katipinimitaoch* look like?"

The magic man stared at Andrew, drew a deep breath and coughed from the harsh fumes of the wood smoke. Then he turned to Pashak.

"You tell the white boy that the antlered man has the head of a huge male caribou and the powerful body of a man," said Cut Cheek. "His long coat is covered with mysterious yet beautiful designs. Later I will paint some for you on the lodge skins in his colors which are blood red and raven black and lynx-eye yellow. He gave me red ocher in a sacred bag," said Cut Cheek. "But I warn you, it is costly! Every form and line I make for you is worth some special gift."

"When will the caribou come?" Mium-scum asked the magic man.

Cut Cheek held his left hand up against his mouth,

his right hand he extended just above the fire. He did not speak until the son's wife, Wapen, laid a pair of mitts and moccasins within his greedy grasp.

"Tomorrow, if the wind is still," said Cut Cheek. "We will separate and hide each family in the winter forest with everyone spread out watching carefully from the hills. Show little smoke and let the women keep the young ones quiet. Tonight we will hold *Mokoshar*, our sacred ritual with the caribou marrow bones. Only when that has been done will the caribou spirit send his children to you—if you observe my every word."

They hunted hard for seven days, but no caribou came to them.

On the eighth night, Mium-scum and the others gave Cut Cheek the last fish that they possessed and listened in the dark without suspicion as he gently tapped the drum. They heard him calling softly.

> "*Now, now, now!*
> *Wide antlers, swift hooves,*
> *Warm-skinned friends,*
> *Come to the true men.*
> *Now, now, now!*"

The only thing that came to them was a tremendous windstorm. It roared out of the North Atlantic Ocean across the dangerous mountains of Labrador. The storm carried with it rain that turned to sleet as it swept across Ungava Bay, covering the inland with a heavy crust of ice. Then snow came burying the stony ridges.

Andrew shuddered as they all sat in the big ice-sheathed tent and listened to what sounded like frightful ghosts and windigoes howling across the tundra plain, rattling the frozen branches of each dwarf black spruce.

"The caribou must have passed to the north or south of us," Mium-scum said. "This morning early I walked out and saw a death sign in the blackened embers of the women's fire."

"They say there is no food left," Pashak told Andrew sadly. "We must leave this hungry place before it is too late."

"Cut Cheek has lost his power," Osken whispered. "He robs trade goods from us, then gives us nothing back but lies."

"Give me my mittens," Wapen screamed at Cut Cheek.

"You did not earn the snare line or the candy," the head packman snarled. "You give them back to us!"

Cut Cheek told them that before he could repay them he wished to go out into the forest and call to all the spirits. Once outside he snatched up his toboggan line and swiftly disappeared, hurrying east to seek more fortunate families. His nervous helper ran behind him.

Wapen said, "I think it's that skinny helper who ties a thong onto the lodge pole and causes it to shake, don't you?"

Pashak did not answer her.

"We must spread out," Mium-scum said. "Each family try to feed itself and stay alive."

Binding on their snowshoes, Wapen and Pashak looked at each other, knowing it might be for the last time. If they survived the winter, they would try to meet again near the singing falls when the geese returned.

The Mium-scum family trailed into the southeast, following the frozen river course, searching desperately for caribou. The others went off in various directions.

With all their food gone, but carrying the company's trade goods, Andrew and Pashak and the packmen left the camp in single file, their dogs dragging their toboggans. Once more they moved southeast along the river, searching for any signs that might lead them to the scattered caribou herd. They might never have survived the journey except that on the second day they saw hundreds of ptarmigan, soft white-feathered birds with furry feet, whose dark rich flesh drove energy into all of them.

Three days later they arrived at Ghost Lake.

"There it is," said Pashak, pointing through the snow-filled trees.

They picked the best site for the outpost, unloaded the toboggans and the heavy packs and built a temporary camp. But they were hungry and without meat.

"If we spread out in all directions, each man searching," the head packman told them, "we should be seeing caribou."

But they found not one. In desperation they chopped holes through the thickening ice and fished for big lake trout. But they took almost none. They hunted hare and ptarmigan, catching only enough to stay alive. Each morning it seemed to Andrew that it could not grow colder. But it did. The cold was so great it split the frozen trees with a noise as sharp as pistol shots.

The packmen, using their snowshoes like hand shovels, cleared away the snow for building, and with the axe and hatchets, they cut and laid out the log foundation for the outpost. It was small, but that would make it easy to keep warm. Using only hatchets and their crooked knives, they split and fashioned one window frame and a sturdy door and frame for the outpost cabin.

The two toboggan drivers were as hardy as the packmen. They fished through the ice in every kind of weather. But without food they all knew they could not stay in such a place.

"They want to help us," Pashak said, "to put up the outpost walls and roof beams and stretch canvas over them until we split some shakes. But they must hurry now or lose their strength."

"There is no one coming here to trade," the packmen said, "except the ghosts of hunger. We are *washkanekan inno,* people who belong near Fort Chimo. Will you not come away with us?"

"You must go. And take the dogs," said Pashak. "There is no food here for them."

"We have decided to stay," said Andrew. "We will find food and we will finish building the outpost."

Next morning Pashak and Andrew waved goodbye to the packers, watching as men and dogs with flat packs and empty toboggans moved quickly out of sight. Andrew could see that they were anxious to leave the enclosed silence of the boreal forest, eager to return to their open homeland and their families once again.

That day Andrew and Pashak worked hard to keep from thinking that they were hungry and utterly alone. Together they cut many small thick trees and stood them around their shelter. They made a spruce bough floor of double thickness and carefully arranged their smoke hole so that it would not draw down the wind. Somewhere out on Ghost Lake they could hear starved wolves howling in a high-pitched chorus of utter misery.

Andrew and Pashak slept fitfully that night, and in the early morning they woke before the light came. They listened in the darkness.

At dawn they fed wood to the fire, drank tea, and tried to think of cheerful things, anything to put out of their minds the stories of powerful dwarfs and ugly-tempered spirits that were said to live in caves beneath the surface of the earth.

"All the time while we were snowshoeing south along the river," Andrew said, "I kept imagining the look of Ghost Lake. I dreamed about it, sometimes seeing it blue and open as in summer."

Pashak laughed. "I usually believe in dreams," he said. "But this Ghost Lake of ours is just one sheet of ice so wide we cannot see across it."

"I used to imagine," said Andrew, "that we would see smoke rising from peaceful Indian villages along its shores, see geese flying and salmon leaping up the falls and watch huge herds of caribou grazing on the open tundra."

"And instead of that," said Pashak, "you have a nightmare all around you. There is not one single track of caribou and we are left alone here, slowly starving. We have all our trade goods piled outside our shelter, but there is no food and not another single human here to trade with."

Four more days they waited. Andrew fished endlessly

and caught only one lean trout. Pashak hunted and caught two ptarmigan. Together they erected a high cache and carefully stored the company's trade goods. A blizzard came and wiped out every sign of tracks.

"When this storm dies, we must leave," said Pashak, "while we still have strength."

In the morning Andrew woke. The violent wind had gone. He saw Pashak sit up in his blankets, holding out his hand so that Andrew, too, would listen.

"What did you hear?" Andrew whispered.

"That's an *uskatcon* calling, a gray robber bird signaling to all the other animals, telling them it sees a human, or something it believes is human."

Pashak pulled on his moccasins and flung his coat across his shoulders. Cautiously raising the entrance flap, he stepped outside, then whispered through the snow-bent wall, "Androoo, Androoo, you come out here quick! I see pale ghosts of humans moving on the lake."

IX

Ghost Lake

ANDREW LEAPED OUT OF HIS BLANKET, PULLED ON HIS knee-length moccasins and hurried out to join Pashak, who stood pointing in horror down the lake. In the drifting ice fog they saw half a dozen moving silver images that seemed to float above the ice.

"Some call this the lake of the dead," Pashak whispered. "We are alone here. There are no living humans wandering out there. I tell you those are ghosts."

"Where is the telescope?" said Andrew.

"It's in the strongbox," said Pashak.

"I'll get it," Andrew whispered. He polished its frosted lenses clean and drew it open carefully, focusing out across the frozen lake.

"I can't see them now," said Pashak. "They're gone. A white man's telescope won't help you see the ghosts."

Andrew searched the ice fog carefully, but the mysterious figures had truly disappeared.

"I guess you're right," said Andrew as he closed the glass.

"Look! Look!" said Pashak. "I can see them again!"

Andrew saw nine of them emerging from the blowing snow.

"Let me look through the glass," said Pashak, and he steadied it on Andrew's shoulder.

"Real humans! Not ghosts at all!" shouted Pashak. "That's the whole Agawan family. My sister Phim should be with them. What could they be doing this far south?"

Pashak snatched his snowshoes down from the spruce branch and tossed Andrew his.

"I want to talk to them, ask them if other families are coming here, ask them where they're going! Hurry, they'll be halfway across the lake before we catch them. The Agawan family is famous for going fast on snowshoes, especially out there on the open lake when the wind is pushing at their backs."

Without packs to weight them down, Pashak and Andrew made good time over the snowy surface of the lake. When they had gone a mile or more Pashak stopped and unlaced his snowshoes.

"Why are you doing that?" asked Andrew.

"Look," said Pashak and he stamped his foot on the snow. "The wind has made it hard as earth. You sling your snowshoes on your back like this," he said, "and we will run in this direction. That way we will go faster and meet the Agawans where they are going."

Andrew found it much easier and faster going, without snowshoes, as they trotted across the hard-packed lake snow.

"We, ourselves, will look like ghosts," said Pashak,

"if they see us running through this ice fog, for it is growing worse."

When they again saw the Agawan family, all nine of them were huddled together with sharp knives drawn to protect themselves.

"It is me, Pashak," he called out to them, "a true man, Pashak, and his friend. We are not wandering spirits."

"Oh, brother of mine!" Andrew heard a girl's voice call out and saw her sheath the short knife in her belt and run across the ice to greet her brother, Pashak.

They both had tears in their eyes when Pashak said to Andrew, "This is my older sister, Phim. She is married to Agawan's son, Sango. She travels with his family."

Phim smiled at Andrew and brushed the dry snow from her brother's leggings.

"You've got sisters wandering all over this country," Andrew said to Pashak. "Each one more beautiful than the other."

"You see only my relatives because there are so few families out here," Pashak replied.

Agawan sheathed his knife and came forward to greet them.

"A strange and lonely meeting place," he said. "We are glad to see that you are well. At first we feared that we saw your dead spirits running toward us. That is why we drew our knives."

"That is not surprising," Pashak said politely. "Why are you hunting so far south?"

"Because we found nothing north of here and we had no food cached. Our hunger drives us here. We saw not a sign of caribou until this morning," Agawan said, "when we saw the tracks of six animals. They are moving around the lake. That is why we were hurrying across to try and cut them off before nightfall. Come and join us."

"We have nothing to hunt with. We did not bring the gun."

"You have knives; that's all you need," said Agawan. "Come on!" And with those words he turned and trotted away, leading all of them across the lake.

Like Andrew and Pashak, the family carried their snowshoes on their backs.

Andrew fancied himself as a good runner, but after a mile he found that he was panting and straining hard to keep up to the adults. The three children were starting to straggle behind, but no one waited for them.

"I can see the other side," gasped Andrew, and he pointed out the low blue shadows of the hills to Pashak.

"Agawan runs as though he knew just where he would meet the caribou."

And indeed he did.

There in the soft snow on the shore of the lake stood all six caribou staring at them. Andrew watched Agawan and his hunters lacing on their snowshoes.

"Where they stand the snow is soft and deep."

"How will we hunt them?" Andrew whispered.

"You will see," said Pashak. "Follow me."

Without another word from anyone, Agawan's wife and their sons' wives, Phim and Shibush, stood up and started waving their arms and singing. Agawan and his two sons, crouching low, moved out to the west.

Pashak and Andrew circled to the east of the caribou. The animals stood, heads up, nervously listening to the women as they sang soothing words to them.

Agawan, his sons, and Pashak and Andrew approached the caribou at the same time, and spreading in a wide circle, they then started shouting. Andrew saw the lead caribou go plunging through the deep snow trying to get past Agawan, who sprang forward on his snowshoes like a giant lynx. Lunging out with his long knife, he stabbed the rearing animal in the heart. The other animals wheeled around in panic and raced straight at Pashak, who crouched, knife drawn, ready to meet them. As the hunters bellowed out in triumph, the women and the three children ran toward them screaming. Not a caribou escaped them.

When he had caught his breath, Agawan and the others raised their arms in thanks for the abundance of food that had been given to them on the very day when their strength was fleeing from them.

The women sharpened their knives against whetstones and swiftly skinned and quartered the caribou before they froze. The men cut spruce and threw up a lodge shelter just big enough for all eleven of them to eat and sleep. They built two roaring fires before the entrance to the lodge and the women, having no pots with them, wrapped long rich strips of meat around birch sticks and stood them upright in the snow so they leaned over the fire. As the meat turned sizzling brown, Andrew saw the fat run down the stick. He, like the others, snatched one up and gobbled down the hot delicious meat.

Stick after stick of meat he ate and laughed with

the others as the warm feeling of food spread through his body once again.

"We should save meat. We shouldn't eat too much," said Andrew.

"Why not?" said Pashak. "It's as easy to carry meat in your belly as it is to carry it on your back. You need rich meat and fat. We all need that. I've been worrying about you, Androoo. You've been growing skinny."

Agawan's wife was named Piwas. She had wild hair and wilder eyes and was known to many as a very clever woman and a powerful storyteller. Both Pashak and his sister Phim urged Piwas to perform a story for Andrew, assuring her that Andrew had never heard a true Naskapi tale.

Perform was the right word to use, for as Piwas told her story, she used a hundred facial expressions and waved her hands until she made the images of spirits dance against the firelight and fly like ghostly shadows along the frosted shelter walls.

Pashak interpreted her tale like this:

Once there was a young child who was always scratching, scratching, scratching. To his parents it looked bad.

Finally the boy's father said to his mother, "We are going inland to hunt with others and I am ashamed of this only child of yours who is always scratching himself. Let us go away alone together. He is worthless. Let us leave him here."

The father repeated, "Worthless, leave him, worthless," until finally next morning the mother agreed.

Both parents took down the tent and went outside and laced on their snowshoes.

"Mother!" the small boy cried. "Are you not going to put on my moccasins?"

His mother did not answer him, but taking up her toboggan strap, she and her husband started off along the frozen river.

"Mother, are you leaving me?" the young boy cried, and tried to run after them.

But his feet were freezing in the snow. He hopped back to the place where their tent had been. The small boy sat crying with his feet in the fire's cold ashes until a ghostly spirit came to him.

"Why did your parents leave you?" the spirit asked him.

"Because I was always scratching, scratching, scratching," said the boy.

"Heat makes you scratch," said the spirit. "Do not sit too close to a hot fire. Would you like to go to your family?"

"Oh, yes," the small boy cried.

So the spirit took him up onto his shoulders and ran through the winter woods with him until they found the place where the boy's family had camped with others. The spirit placed him down outside his father's tent and the little boy went inside.

The mother looked at him in fright and said, "Husband, can this be our son whom we abandoned? How could he have come all this way along the frozen river in his bare feet?"

"Who brought you here?" the father asked his son.

"My grandfather," said the boy.

"Where is he now?" the father asked.

"He is sitting outside your tent."

"You go and look outside," the boy's father said to his wife.

The boy's mother raised the tent flap and looked outside. "Yes," she said, "there is somebody sitting out there."

The old ghost spirit stuck his head inside the tent and said, "You call me 'somebody' but I say that you are 'nobody' to have left your child to perish!"

The boy's father begged his own father's spirit to come inside the tent, but it refused until the small boy went outside and took his grandfather's ghost by the hand and led it into the tent. Together the four of them slept peacefully around the fire.

In the morning all the people were going out to hunt caribou and they asked the young boy, whom they believed was magic, to come with them. Before he left, the boy offered to bring back to his grandfather's spirit some especially tasty pieces of caribou. His grandfather's ghost told him exactly which pieces he preferred.

That night the boy returned on his small snowshoes. In his backpack were the choice pieces of meat that his grandfather desired.

"Where is he?" the boy asked his mother.

She answered only, "Your father's father has gone."

At dawn the small boy followed his grandfather's snowshoe tracks, which led across a frozen lake. When he saw his grandfather's pale spirit moving slowly through the ice fog, he cried out to him, "Grandfather, Grandfather! I have the choicest pieces saved for you!"

"You keep them, grandson," the spirit cried out to him. "I can no longer stay among the living people." And he disappeared.

Sadly the boy returned to camp and told his family that he would again go searching for his grandfather. But on the following day a storm arose and the snow-shoe tracks of his grandfather were drifted over. The small boy could no longer follow him or lead his grandfather's spirit back from the other world.

When the story was ended, they all lay down together and slept like exhausted children through the night, not hearing or caring about the wolves that came and tore at the scraps of caribou beyond their fire.

In the morning, Agawan said to Pashak and to Andrew, "Join us. Come with us. I believe we will find more caribou south of here. Those we took yesterday will not last my family and the two of you for even half a moon. I have sent my two sons back for our tent and toboggan and the other things we have with us."

Andrew and Pashak gladly agreed to hunt with them. Together they ran back across the lake and loaded a few things on the one toboggan left them by the pack-men. Working together, each with a long line, they pulled it across the lake. They were glad that all the dogs had returned with the packmen. There would have been no way for them to feed them.

Piwas, Shibush and Pashak's sister, Phim, had all the meat cut for easy loading on the two toboggans. Traveling in single file they snowshoed far south of Ghost Lake. The snow grew deeper and the stands of spruce and birch increased. Once Andrew followed a rabbit track, noticing that suddenly its length of jumps increased and its trail zigzagged crazily until it vanished altogether.

"Why is that?" asked Andrew. "No tracks are following that rabbit."

"None that you see," said Pashak. "Like magic the rabbit tracks disappear."

"Where did he go?" said Andrew.

"He took off and flew," Pashak answered. "An owl helped him with its claws hooked in that frightened rabbit's back."

"I've got a lot to learn," said Andrew.

"So have I." Pashak smiled at Andrew.

"Look there and over there," said Pashak on the fifth morning of their southern wanderings. "That's a marten's track, and that's a fisher's and there's the small track of a mink. We are entering into rich fur country. See that windswept river ice that shines before you? That is the southern boundary of Naskapi country. Beyond that river stand the mountains. You can see them in the distance wrapped in pale blue shadows. We scarcely know the mountain people," Pashak said to Andrew. "Many fear them, saying it is best to keep away. They are very different than ourselves."

That night when they made camp Agawan's wife Piwas said aloud so everyone of them could hear, "I am not afraid to cross that river. My oldest brother told me that he crossed here when I was still a young child riding in a moss-filled pouch. My brother was with three *Nenenat* families. They met the mountain men. Yet none of them were harmed."

"I have heard of families that have journeyed south of that river and have not returned," said Sango. "They say that these mountain people are very cruel."

"Their mountain country is said to teem with every kind of game animal," said Agawan. "Black bears and caribou and lynx, and marten, fisher, fox, and many kinds of useful birds and fish. These worthy animals surely would not give themselves to cruel and worthless folk."

"I believe that what Agawan says is true," said Pashak, "even though my grandfather, Natiwapio, warned me that I must be oh so careful if I ever found myself near mountain people."

Next morning, they cautiously crossed the river before daylight and moved silently into the country of the Montagnais, for that name had been given the inhabitants by the French. They traveled south through rolling country crisscrossed with a thousand animal tracks. But having meat on their toboggans, the Agawan family did not hunt.

That night Piwas said, "Did you not feel it, husband? Did none of you feel human eyes upon you? Toward evening I was sure that we were being watched by someone."

"You're making stories," said her husband. "You're only imagining that. Don't say such things."

But that night when Andrew went outside, he saw a movement in the moon's long shadows and thought perhaps he saw a bear. But when he looked more closely, he could see that it was a man with a rifle moving cautiously between the dwarf black trees, crouching so that he would not be seen.

X

Mountain Folk

ANDREW STEPPED INSIDE THE TENT AND TOLD PASHAK that he had seen a strange man who tried to hide from him. Pashak looked closely at Andrew and said, "Maybe you saw the shadow of a tree branch swaying in the wind."

Next morning when they went outside their tent, the air was cold without a breath of wind. Andrew showed Pashak and Agawan the strange man's snowshoe tracks.

"He is not carrying a heavy pack, so he camps not far from here," said Pashak.

"Yes, that is so," said Agawan. "But I see something puzzling. He wears his snowshoes backwards, trying to make us believe that he is going north instead of south."

"Is he a Naskapi?" Andrew asked them.

"Of course not," Agawan answered pointing at the

track. "No true man's wife would weave a web like that."

The Agawan family, with Pashak and Andrew, traveled no great distance south before they saw the thin white smoke of four fires rising straight as arrows into the cold blue sky.

"I am afraid," said Phim. She clutched her two children to her. "Should we not go back across our river?"

"No," said Agawan. "We men will go straight to their camp and tell them why we have come. We should take the guns with us, loaded, but leave them on the toboggans. We will hide our knives in our leggings. This tent we will leave here with the women and the children."

"I am nervous of the eyes I felt last night," said Piwas, "and of the rifleman who wears his snowshoes backwards to deceive us."

"Silence woman! We have made our plan!" said Agawan.

Andrew and Pashak and the other men followed him south to a point where they could look across into a protective fold in the hills and see two long birchbark-covered lodges almost hidden by the bending branches of the soft white forest. The first real sign of life they saw was when a woman stepped out of the nearest lodge and hung a round-stretched beaver skin upon a tree branch. Then a man and a boy came out and stood a fallen toboggan upright in the snow.

"*Ha-wah-ho!*" Agawan called out to them.

The man pushed the woman and the boy back inside the lodge while he alone crouched near the entrance staring up at the strangers in terrified suspicion. It was not long before six other mountain men appeared behind him. All of them were carrying weapons—rifles and shotguns—which they held ready against the Naskapi hunters.

Agawan and the others pulled back their sleeves and, holding out their hands, said, "We are not ghosts. We carry no weapons. We come to you peacefully as friends, ones who are in trouble."

The Montagnais whispered to each other for a moment, then stood their weapons upright in the snow and made the same sign to these men from the north.

"Be careful when they come near you," the mountain headman whispered to the others. "I don't like those wild people sneaking into our land, no matter what their reasons."

Then their headman called, "Come forward and we will speak together."

Even to Andrew the Montagnais dialect sounded sharp and strange, but since they all spoke the northern Algonquin tongue, they could understand each other, though at first just barely.

When they were a dozen paces from the Montagnais lodge, the headman called out, "*Tshekwan;* what do you want?"

"The caribou have failed us," Agawan answered him. "We have suffered terrible ice storms in the north and we believe that many of our people will starve before spring comes to us again. Almost no caribou have been seen in our whole country. We were forced to move south to you, or die."

The headman whispered to the other hunters, then said, "Here we have animals and meat aplenty. The winter moons have been good to us. Our young people living here have never known such great abundance. The hills to the southeast are decorated with countless caribou tracks. These cross the trails of many other animals. We will be glad to share our country's bounty with you—for a little while."

Andrew could see the Montagnais women and children moving cautiously out from the entrance of their two long lodges. These mountain folk looked strange to him in their tall, conical red and blue French-style hats and long, loose coats and leggings, with many silver beads and brooches pinned onto their clothing.

One of their women called out something Andrew could not understand.

Pashak said, "She wants to know if we have women and children with us."

Agawan answered, "Yes."

"Then go and get them," said their headman. "Bring them back with you. We will prepare a feast. Let every person lay aside his weapons. Come and eat and sleep with us."

"They do not sound like bad people," Piwas said to Agawan, when he repeated all that they had said. "But still, husband, I will find it difficult to lie down near them and close my eyes to sleep."

For five nights and days the Agawans, with Andrew and Pashak, and the mountain folk feasted together, sleeping whenever they felt like sleeping, enjoying the strange mountain drumming and their storytelling and the singing. Pashak told Andrew that his sister Phim had told him she wished it would never end.

On the sixth day, a strange thing happened. The work dogs gave warning and a huge black bear came shambling through the forest near their camp. The Montagnais men and their women sang praise songs to the bear. Their hunters, who seemed confident that the bear would not run away, did an elaborate dance in his honor before they went forth to make him theirs.

Andrew and Pashak followed the mountain men but took no part in the hunt. They watched the Montagnais hunters lash their long-bladed daggers onto wooden shafts. Holding these spears, they surrounded the bear, still singing to him.

The bear rose up on his hind feet and stood threatening them as though he were a man disguised in his glossy blue-black coat.

"Forgive me, *macwah*," said their headman as he drew back his dagger spear and dealt the powerful beast a single deadly thrust.

When the rich sweet bear meat was simmering in the pots, the mountain folk gladly shared a last great feast with the "wild ones."

When all of them could eat no more, the true men watched while the Montagnais reverently boiled the bear skull until its bones turned white as snow. With great care they decorated the bear's forehead with sacred spots of rich red ocher mixed with lines of azure blue. At dawn, with ceremonious singing and with ponderous bearlike dancing, the mountain hunters wedged the bear skull firmly in a tree crotch. Each one bid the sacred head a fond farewell.

For three days following the bear feast, the Montagnais fasted, eating nothing save a little snow to ease their thirst. Each night they drummed and danced until dawn came, then slept all through the day.

"I'm not used to such strange goings on," said Agawan's wife. "Husband, don't you think it is time for us to leave this foreign place?"

With Piwas's words their long visit ended.

It was the sixth day of the waning winter moon. The Montagnais abandoned their birch-bark lodges, saying, "Use them if you wish, but do not touch the dear bear's skull."

Hurriedly the mountain folk packed up their huge bales of fur on one long toboggan and their meat and back fat on the other and began their annual journey south to the Saint Lawrence River.

"We must travel south while the snow is firm," their headman said. "We wish to do our trading with the French who live along the mighty river."

"Now I trust those mountain people," Piwas said. "I like their women. They are kindly. And their men are good providers. Did you see their women's heavy strings of lovely beads and silver buttons?"

"They speak our language strangely," Pashak's sister said. "I enjoyed their company and their bear meat stew more than their weird way of dancing. I hope they will come north across our river and feast with us sometime," said Phim.

"Can you imagine why those mountain people build their lodges in the strange way they do and carry their babies in birchbark baskets on their backs"—Piwas laughed—"instead of using nice, soft, moss-filled caribou bags as we do? The only thing I mind about the Montagnais is that they gave us the name "wild people." Imagine them calling us wild people when I would say *they* are the wild ones." Piwas shuddered. "Did you hear the rude words of the songs they sing?"

"Women should not gossip about those who shared their food with us," said Agawan.

"It was nice of them to leave these two bark lodges to us," Piwas said, "but still, I don't like them. Their lodges are far too dark inside. I like our bright tents where the sunlight comes through the canvas and through our well-cleaned skins."

When they were ready to leave, Pashak stripped the wide sheets of birchbark from one lodge and rolled them carefully.

"Why are you doing that?" asked Andrew.

"It is useful. They brought this bark from the south. We don't have good wide bark up here. Our trees are small."

That same day they harnessed their toboggans and eagerly moved into the low-wooded hills to the east. As the mountain men had promised, the hills were crisscrossed with caribou tracks and they could see whole herds of them lying on the hillsides. They killed only those they could eat, and they were more than thankful for the meat.

Pashak said to Andrew, "This may be our only chance to take some fur."

Both men and women set out traps and snares and built many clever deadfalls. They caught mink, marten, otter, beaver, fox and fisher in great numbers. The women stayed up half the nights stretching and drying the precious skins. The three children laughed and did all their hopping games and played snow snakes, a game where each person tries to throw a long thin stick straight along a track dug in the snow and make it jump when it reaches an icy mound.

"There are frozen beaver ponds just east of here," said Pashak. "Let us go and see if we can find their lodges."

Together Andrew and Pashak made a narrow snowshoe trail that led through the sparse forest and rolling foothills. When they arrived at the ponds, they found many beaver lodges. They built a lean-to of thick spruce and spent the night.

In the morning Pashak said, "A man came here and watched us as we slept."

"Where?" said Andrew.

"There. Quite close. But now he's gone off, traveling west. I followed his tracks. You can see his trail stretch way across the hills. He's gone."

They followed backward along his old trail that led among the beaver lodges. Then Pashak and Andrew separated to see how they would place their stakes and raise the water level to trap the beaver.

As Andrew knelt beside a beaver lodge and listened, he had an uneasy feeling and, looking up, he saw a man dressed in a moose hide coat with dangling fringes. On his head he wore a lynx-skin cap with long tufted ears. It made him look inhuman, like a cat. For a long moment they stared at each other, neither moving. Then slowly the stranger raised his rifle and pointed it at Andrew's head.

XI

Night Thief

"ROLL!" SCREAMED PASHAK, AND ANDREW FLUNG HIMSELF sideways as he heard the gun explode and saw the snow leap up beside him.

Pashak, with his knife out, went bounding across the clearing. But the stranger slipped away and disappeared between the snow-laden spruces. Together they followed him but only for a little way.

"That was the man you saw who had his snowshoes tied on backwards."

"Why would he have fired at me?"

"Well," said Pashak, "we are in strange country, not our country."

"But," said Andrew, "their headman told us we could hunt here."

"Yes," said Pashak, "but others do not know that. Headmen in any country often disagree. Hurry," Pashak urged him. "I want to reach our camp before he finds the women."

When they told Agawan all that had happened, he said, "It's time for us to move. Let's go and cross the river into our own country. There we will set up camp away from this lynx-headed killer who wears his snow-shoes backwards and has no respect for human life."

They moved across the river and were astonished to find that the animals had also crossed and were there in even greater numbers. Still, their troubles were not over. In the moment of their greatest plenty their camp was discovered by a raiding wolverine.

They didn't see the brute, but they found his tracks and saw the awful things that he had done to their meat cache.

Fearing that wolves might come, Agawan had hung all their caribou meat in trees. But that did not foil the wolverine. He leaped into the lower branches, chewed through all the thongs and dropped all the fattest haunches on the snow. He had stuffed himself with as much as his belly would hold, then spat and clawed and urinated on all of the remaining meat. After that he tore the fur stretchers down from the trees and ripped the precious skins to pieces. When everything was destroyed, he wandered off in triumph to sleep in his clever hiding place until his hunger woke him and drove him forth to carry out some new destruction.

Agawan and Sango and their wives and even the children raged against the wolverine.

"He's not just an animal," Pashak said to Andrew. "He's an evil spirit sent to ruin us, to destroy everything we own."

Both Pashak and Agawan sat up all that night hidden near the remnants of their meat cache with shotguns resting across their knees. But the cunning wolverine only watched them and, using its keen senses, stayed well away from them.

The next night before they slept, they carefully built a heavy log deadfall and set out wire snares and cruel-jawed wolf traps. The sly wolverine came raiding once again. In the morning Andrew followed its long-clawed footprints, seeing where the animal had gone to every trap and snare and sprung it, who knows how? Then it had gone to the heavy deadfall, and with one clever claw had released its wooden trigger, causing it to crash down harmlessly. Only after that had the wolverine felt free to tear apart and leave its stench on the last of their caribou meat. Before dawn came the wolverine had scattered their cache of fish and birds, destroying everything.

"We will have to get rid of that beast or move away from here," said Agawan after his third sleepless night of waiting when the cautious wolverine refused to come.

Perhaps we should move," Andrew said. "This wolverine is not like that stranger with a rifle. This one will not follow us."

"Don't be too sure of that," said Piwas. "Wolverines are far more cunning than most animals or humans." She paused and said, "I believe that I can rid you of this evil one."

"That I would like to see." Agawan laughed.

Piwas called to Pashak's sister. "Phim, you soak this piece of cloth with that strong perfume my son bought you at the trade store. Then tie the smelly thing around a stone that is just right sized for a woman's throwing. Husband," she said, "give me that little bag of white fish roe that you use to mix your paints." She smelled it and wrinkled up her nose. "Smells terrible! Just right to drown out the human smell of my mitts and hands." "Pashak," she said, handing him a piece of caribou meat, "you chew this until it's soft and well ground up. Be careful, hungry boy, don't swallow any."

While Andrew and the others watched her, Agawan's wife took up the thigh bone of a caribou and with the small axe struck its end, causing a long thin strip of bone to splinter off. Piwas took the long bone sliver in her hands and bent it like a small bow, then let it go and watched it spring back straight. Carefully she took a knife and sharpened both ends of the bone into deadly arrow points.

"Now bring the meat outside," she said to Pashak.

She stepped outside the tent and all the others followed her. Carefully she coiled the bending piece of bone until it rested in her hand like a strong clock spring. She took the chewed-up piece of meat from Pashak in her mitted hand and into it she carefully pressed the arrow-pointed coil of bone with her fish roe scented hand. She held the meat out until it stiffened and froze in the cold night air.

"There," she said examining the weapon she had created.

"Now," she said to Pashak's sister, "if you have that strong smelling perfume cloth tied round the stone, you throw it as far as you can, way over there." She pointed to a smooth snow-covered place among the trees where none of them had ever walked.

When Agawan's wife saw the perfumed stone land and slither across the crust, she drew back her arm and threw the piece of meat so that it landed somewhere near the stone.

"Why did she do that?" asked Andrew.

"She says if we come inside she'll tell you. Outside she's afraid the wolverine will hear her words and stay away."

Even inside the tent Agawan's wife whispered her words. "Wolverines are oh so wise and careful, but like humans they are curious too.

"When the wolverine smells that strong perfume, he will wonder what it is and go over there. Seeing that there are no human footprints and no traps or snares or deadfalls set for him, he will feel safe. Of course, he will be far too cautious to touch the strange smelling stone. But near it he will find our innocent scrap of meat that has a delicious fishy smell."

"What then?" said Andrew.

"Who knows what then." Agawan's wife laughed. "It is a woman's trick. Phim and I will go out early in the morning. Perhaps we will bring him home to you."

"I can't believe my eyes!" said Pashak as he held open the tent flap for Agawan and everyone to see.

Trailing across the snow toward them came Piwas and Phim on snowshoes. Piwas had a skin line across her shoulder and was dragging the huge carcass of the wolverine behind her. It was as big as a small bear, with short powerful legs and long dangerously hooked claws. Its lips were wrinkled back beneath its snub nose in a horrible frozen snarl that showed its enormous yellow teeth. Its tail was short and its hide was coarse and thick, with bushy hair marked like a skunk and long, black and tan fur.

"How did they ever catch him?" Andrew asked Pashak in amazement.

"He caught himself, the greedy thing," said Piwas. "We saw his tracks. He went first to the perfumed stone and circled it, then found our frozen ball of meat and swallowed it in one great gulp. He tried to climb a tree to reach our best marten skins but halfway up the trunk he stopped. Why? Because that meat ball in his stomach thawed and released my double arrow. It sprung straight open and pierced him in the heart. This wolverine," she said, "won't steal our meat again, or tear our other furs to pieces."

XII

Desperate Journey

ON THE VERY DAY THAT THE HARD-FACED WINTER MOON
had disappeared, they waxed the toboggans and pre-
pared for their long march north toward Fort Chimo.
They gathered all the meat and fur that they could
haul with them.

"Women, women! Take down the tent," said Agawan.
"This is our day of leaving. When the sun is high we
shall begin our journey homeward following the
crooked river."

At the end of their first day's march they stood outside their tent and watched as the pale, thin curve
of the new spring moon was born again and rose into
the star-filled sky.

"I cannot tell you why," said Pashak, "but somehow I have a longing to race north as fast as my legs
will carry me. To paddle hard, to run, to leap, to jump,
to spread my wings and fly back to Fort Chimo. I can
scarcely wait for the summer feasting and to see the

nitiomosetts—beloved girls—come running to the sound
of drumming and of dancing. I have never felt this way
before in all my life."

"I know what you mean," said Andrew. "I, too, feel
like dancing in the snow."

"Have you ever thought of getting married, Androoo?"

"Nooo!" said Andrew. "It's too soon for me to think
of silly things like that."

"Not for me, it's not." Pashak laughed. "I think of
getting married all the time, especially when we are
heading for the fort for summer feastings."

On the following morning Pashak rushed inside the
wigwam and shook Andrew.

"It's warm outside and I hear spruce hens calling."

The hunters laughed, turned somersaults and did
wild spring dances in the melting snow. They spoke of
all the wondrous things that they would trade for at
the white man's fort.

"Spring has arrived! Feel the softness in the air. I
swear to you that summer is on its way!"

"I think you're right," said Andrew and he, too, did
his version of a Scottish sword dance.

Like a sky canoe the half moon sailed through long
white waves of clouds at night and in the midday sun
the frozen river's surface turned to melting slush. That
was why the Agawan family slept all day and traveled
at night and watched the moon wax full, then start to
wane again before they reached the singing falls. Each
day grew warmer as the sun gained strength and caused
the sun-warmed rocks to push their way up through
the snow. Andrew's face turned red then brown as
Pashak's. Even early in the mornings the travelers drew

black charcoal circles round their eyes to keep from going snowblind. Plump white ptarmigan were everywhere, flashing their white wings and calling "Come-ear! Come-ear!" as they flew over the patches of open tundra searching for mates.

"I still worry about the other families," Piwas said. "For days now we have moved through the whole country without seeing a single caribou or human snowshoe track."

They pulled their long toboggans north and watched the trees dwindle and the low blue mountains fade behind them.

When they reached the height of land, Agawan pointed northward to a cloud of steam that rose in the clear May morning.

"There is the singing falls, the water is open at the falls. The winter ice is broken there! Listen, you can hear the roar. Let us sleep only a little, then hurry down and meet our relatives," said Agawan. "I can scarcely wait to see our people!"

They arrived in the early morning and pitched their wigwam not far from the roaring falls. Agawan and his sons, with Pashak and Andrew, looked everywhere for snowshoe tracks, or for any human signs. But there were none.

"They should be here by now," said Agawan.

"I am afraid for all of them," said Pashak. "But most of all I worry about my sister Wapen. I had hoped to find her here with all the others."

"We must be patient." Agawan sighed. "We will stay here and fish and wait for them. If they have the strength to come to us, then they will surely come. We cannot search for them, for we would not know whether to look to the east or west or north or south, since there is not a snowshoe track in this whole country round us."

Next evening, just as the Dog Star first appeared, Pashak and his sister Phim, who was as worried as himself, climbed up onto the highest hill and spied carefully with the telescope along the shadowy valleys and the opening river courses, hoping to see some line of tracks or the distant smoke of a campfire, any sign of human life. Except for the bad luck of having a huge snowy owl fly past them, they saw no living thing. The whole country lay shrouded in blue silence stretching endlessly northward to the mist-hung loneliness of Ungava Bay.

"I am so afraid because we saw that owl." Phim wept. "Seeing it makes me afraid for Wapen and for all the others," she told Piwas and Shibush, when they returned to camp.

In the newly opened water beyond the falls, Pashak and Andrew helped Agawan set a clever net, while they themselves used strange-shaped hooks. They caught more fish than they could eat, which, of course, was their intention.

"Hide them carefully," Agawan said. "Be patient. Some of the others will surely come to us. We will need extra food to give them. I think they must be hungry, perhaps starving."

Pashak dug a long trench in the snow beside the river and in it he and Andrew carefully laid out thirty huge trout side by side. Phim brought fresh cold water from the falls and poured it evenly over all of the fish.

In the morning it was as though the trout lay enclosed in clear, thick window glass made of solid ice.

Andrew saw tracks where a whole family of wolves had come and scratched and gnawed at the ice but had failed to rob them of a single fish.

Although Pashak and Phim and Andrew watched each day, Phim's sharp-eyed husband, Sango, was the first to see a lonely figure in the moonlight staggering along the river's edge. He called out to the others, and Pashak and Andrew leaped onto their snowshoes and followed him toward the ghost or human. They approached cautiously with daggers drawn to find that it was Cut Cheek, the shaman, gaunt and weeping, leaning on a staff to help support himself. When he saw them, he collapsed on the snow and told them he was dying from starvation.

Pashak ran back for a toboggan and they pulled him into camp and laid him down on a spruce bough bed of double thickness, and the women rolled him in two blankets and fed him hot thick soup and slippery chunks of fish. At first they did not ask him what had happened, for they could see that he was so thin and his eyes so dull from hunger that he looked more like a skeleton than a human. When they asked about his skinny helper he just looked away and did not answer them.

When Cut Cheek had rested and had been fed again, Pashak whispered to him, "Have you seen the others? Have you seen my sister Wapen, who is married into the Mium-scum family?"

Slowly the shaman raised his trembling hand and pointed eastward. "Their camp is two days journey down the river. They can no longer move, for they are starving."

Andrew and Pashak took the axe and antler ice chisel,

ran down and swiftly chipped open the ice cache. Phim helped them rope up two heavy packs of lake trout weighing almost a hundred pounds apiece. They laced on their snowshoes, slung the big packs on their backs and departed long before dawn, with Pashak breaking trail and Andrew following.

They went along the river's bank. They could not trust their weight upon the rotting ice, for it had been worn thin by treacherous undercurrents. Plodding eastward, rolling his powerful body like a wiry weasel, Pashak drove his snowshoes forward, sinking with every step from his heavily loaded pack. They seldom stopped to rest and even when they did, neither of them removed his heavy pack of fish, but rested it against the rocks along the river bank. The vision of his starving sister, Wapen, drove Pashak forward at a terrible pace, one that Andrew did not believe he could follow. But he did.

No matter how fast Pashak hurried on his wide beaver-tail snowshoes, he could hear Andrew coming right behind him.

"Let me break trail for a while," said Andrew. "You can't do all the hardest work."

Gladly Pashak stepped aside and let Andrew take the lead. They went that way along the river's edge until the evening star appeared.

"We've got to stop," gasped Pashak as he slumped against a tree.

"Oh, I'm glad you said that." Andrew was sobbing. "I can scarcely take another step."

Together they rested their packs against a rock. Then when their breath returned, they slipped off their heavy burdens. They built a spruce bough lean-to, for they had brought no tent.

Andrew awoke at dawn and saw Pashak bending like an old man tying up his moccasins.

"You look the way I feel," said Andrew as he struggled out of his blankets.

They shared some dried pemmican from Andrew's pack. Traveling slowly at first, Pashak broke their snowshoe trail along the river's bank. Andrew could tell by the length of Pashak's strides that he was in a desperate hurry. To save their strength and breath they scarcely spoke to each other.

It was almost dark when they rounded a cove in the river, and suddenly they could see the camp.

"There's no smoke, no sign of life," said Pashak.

Everything looked dead. Andrew stopped and felt fear rise up in him. Would they find poor Wapen and the others starved to death, he wondered? The cold and lifeless camp seemed to stare with hollow eyes at both of them.

XIII

Starvation Cove

THE NIGHT BREEZE DRIFTED SLOWLY DOWN THE RIVER. When it reached the stricken camp, it pressed against the rotting canvas of the old and tattered tents, causing the side walls to breathe in and out with eerie, ghostlike movements that produced a gasping, dying sound.

Andrew and Pashak stumbled into the very center of the camp, reeling with tiredness as they dropped their heavy packs. There was not the slightest sign of human life, not even the smell of long-dead smoke.

"*Wotshimao, wotshimao?*" Pashak called out asking for the headman. Old Mium-scum did not answer. There was only silence.

Pashak seemed too horrified to move, so Andrew pulled back the flap on the first tent and stepped inside. It was dark and cold.

"Mium-scum?" he whispered. "Osken? Wapen? Someone in this tent, please answer me."

He was greeted only by a frozen silence. As Andrew's eyes became accustomed to the gloom, he saw the forms of several persons huddled underneath their blankets. He reached out and touched one of them. The body beneath the blanket was as stiff as stone. Andrew gasped and hurried out of the tent.

Pashak, fearing the worst, leaped toward the other tent and called out, "Wapen! Wapen!"

He pulled back the entrance flap, and as he did so, they both heard a small child's voice whimpering in terror, and a young woman's voice cried weakly, "*Tskhekwan?* Who is it? What do you want?"

"Wapen, don't be afraid. It is me, Pashak, and Androoo."

It was dark, but they could see a human moving and heard the child cry out again.

"Brother, am I dreaming or is that truly you?" Wapen lay sobbing.

"Yes," said Pashak and his voice choked in his throat. "I'm so glad you're still alive."

There was a pause. Then his sister said in a low voice, "Wapen is dying—dying. Will you say goodbye to me?"

So weak was she that she could not sit up but simply lay there weeping helplessly, while she stared up at her brother and held the young child to her.

"Put our blankets around them," said Andrew in a trembling voice, "and I'll build up this fire."

"Pashak, Pashak, say goodbye to me," Wapen said again.

"Don't try to talk," said Pashak.

"I am going," Wapen said in a broken voice. "Oh, Pashak, have you not some scrap of meat for me to take with me?" She moved her lips in a desperate way that shadowed her hollow cheek bones.

"Androoo is making a fire," said Pashak. "We'll boil some fish for you."

"Oh, don't wait. I can't wait! Give me food now or I will faint again."

Pashak cut off a piece of frozen fish and tried to partly thaw it with his hands. Wapen reached out and snatched it from him, her icy fingers hooked like claws. As she stuffed the fish chunk in her mouth, she tore off a shred and gave it to the child, who screamed at the sudden unbelievable thrill of tasting food again.

When the fire in the tent was roaring and had spread its light and warmth, the deep hoarfrost crystals on the inside of the canvas walls began to shimmer, then drip and run away in nervous rivulets. The fish fat simmered in the pot, turned a thick rich yellow and spread like glistening butter over the delicious-smelling soup.

Pashak held his sister in his arms and fed her gently while Andrew knelt and fed the small child.

"We should not give them too much at first or it will make them sick," said Pashak. "I wonder that there are only the two of them alone in this tent."

"Osken went hunting with Macwah," Wapen told him. "They could scarcely walk, but they went out hunting for us. Two days later," she said, "Mium-scum went staggering after them, dragging an empty toboggan. He is old but he is strong, and he never gives up hope. They have all been gone for I don't know how long." Wapen wept. "I don't know how many days we two have been lying here without a fire. If I had not had this child to warm me, we both would have frozen.

Where are all the others? Where is my husband, Osken? Is he lying somewhere out there in the snow?"

"We will look for them," said Pashak. "You sleep now and we will eat again when you wake. We can talk tomorrow."

When Wapen was asleep, Pashak whispered. "Is there no one alive in the other tent?"

Sadly Andrew shook his head.

Pashak went outside in the moonlight, then held up the flap and beckoned to Andrew.

"Put on your snowshoes," he said. "Those must be the tracks of all three of them leading inland. I can tell that one's Mium-scum's," he said, pointing, "because it is an old man's way of walking and he is the one dragging the toboggan."

They wolfed down some of the fish themselves, then made up two small packs and left all the rest close to Wapen. Then together they followed the moonlit trail throughout the night.

In the first light of morning, they saw that the tracks led to a small rude shelter. A thin wisp of smoke was rising through the cut spruce boughs.

"*Wotshimao! Wotshimao! First man!*" Pashak called out from a distance, not wishing to frighten whoever lay inside.

"It is I," an old voice answered, and Mium-scum came slowly crawling out on his hands and knees.

When he saw them, he chuckled and gave them a toothless grin. "I am old," he said, "but I wanted to stay alive to see if you would come. If you have food, please give it to me and I shall stuff it into Osken's mouth. He is only just alive and can no longer crawl.

My poor son Macwah died," said Mium-scum, "and with our last strength we put his body to rest up in that tree."

They fed bits of fish and broth to Osken and to Mium-scum, built up the fire and fixed the shelter. Next day, because they could not wait, they tied Mium-scum and Osken onto the toboggan. Together Pashak and Andrew harnessed themselves and dragged the two starved men back to the camp, where they had left Wapen and the child all alone. Long before they reached the tents they could smell fish soup and they were surprised to see both Wapen and the child outside tending a large pot over a blazing fire.

Wapen wept when she saw her husband Osken and said, "I never gave up hope that you would come back to me again."

Andrew and Pashak waited there for nine days. Wapen and Osken, old Mium-scum and the small girl fleshed out their bones by eating good fat trout and snow geese. The river ice was flooded and the snow faded all around them. The first star-shaped flowers bloomed on the river banks and many birds came flocking from the south to build their nests. Long pin-tailed ducks whirled down into the ponds calling, *Akee-ak-un-nuk! Akke-ak-un-nuk!* Huge stretches of open tundra turned a new gray-green. The last snow clung in the shadows of the trees and caused shimmering mirages in the noonday sun.

"We must leave today," said Pashak, "or we will have too little snow to travel."

As they went down the embankment, they turned and looked back sadly at the dead who rested in the trees.

Old Mium-scum called out, "Farewell, farewell. I never thought that I would be the one to walk away from this starvation cove."

Sometimes Mium-scum rested and allowed them to pull him on the toboggan with the small girl, who still weighed almost nothing. But mostly Mium-scum snowshoed with the others. Food, work and the warm spring sun seemed to bring new life into all their minds and bodies. Still, it seemed a miracle that some of them had returned alive to join the others of the Agawan camp that stood beside the ice-hung falls.

XIV

River Runners

ANDREW AWOKE AND LISTENED TO THE RUMBLING OF THE falls that filled the morning air with the joyful sound of spring, now that the river was freed from its winter prison of ice.

"The river is singing," Pashak's sister called to them, "and the willow ptarmigan are flocking in from the south. They say old Cut Cheek has gone walking, gone to find the place where he and Mium-scum left their good canoes."

Pashak and Andrew jumped out of their blankets, dressed and hurried outside. The sky above the tent was a deep, clear, cloudless blue.

"This is the morning to find the old canoe that Mium-scum has given us," said Pashak. "It is over on the other side."

Using a staff to test the ice, they cautiously crossed the rotting river ice a safe distance above the falls.

"It won't be easy to find," Pashak warned Andrew.

"Mium-scum will have covered it to protect it from the weather."

"There's a paddle," Andrew said, "or half a paddle." He picked it up.

"The porcupines have eaten through the handle," Pashak said. "The last man to handle that must have had fish or caribou fat on his hands. Porcupines search for any kind of grease in winter."

"The canoe must be near the paddle."

And so it was, resting upside down on a low rack almost under Andrew's hand. It was so well covered with old tree bark they might have missed it if they had not seen the paddle.

"We can't use this canoe," said Andrew, when they stripped the old bark away. "Its canvas is rotted through."

"That's why I carried that roll of new birch bark from the Mountain People's country," Pashak said. "We have a few birch trees here, but they are too small to use their bark to cover a canoe. We will heat the bark and then unroll it and tomorrow we will start to work."

Together they stripped the useless canvas from the canoe, then picked up its gray-ribbed skeleton and carried it across the river to the flat, clear piece of ground that stood before their tent. Next morning it was pouring rain.

"Rain's a sign of good luck when you're covering a canoe," said Pashak, "and besides, it will spread pools of water on the ice and open up the river."

Pashak took two pieces of the birchbark and cut them with a head hole so they fitted over his and Andrew's shoulders like a pair of neck yokes.

"Now you won't get wet when we're working,"

Pashak said. "Birchbark is not only waterproof, but it's good for making dozens of different things."

With Agawan helping them, Andrew was surprised at how quickly they were able to fit and sew the bark in place, and by the time they were finished, Agawan's wife, Piwas, and Pashak's sister had gathered and melted pine pitch on the fire. This they spread with care along every sewn bark seam.

In the morning the canoe was ready for the water. As if by magic the rain had eaten into the remaining ice, opening the river as far as they could see.

Sango had secretly been working hard behind the tent. He had split two pieces of hard white birch with his axe and had cut them into size and shape with his sharp crooked knife. When Andrew went in back of the tent, he found Sango finishing two strong paddles as a gift for them.

Sango unwrapped a small piece of broken window glass that he had saved since Chimo, and cracking the glass to make it razor sharp, he scraped both paddle blades as smooth as ice.

"That one's yours," said Sango handing Andrew the longer paddle.

"Is that because I'm tall?" asked Andrew.

"No," said Pashak. "Sango says yours is long because you will be the bowman needing length to push us away from any rocks. My paddle is shorter, wider, because I'll be in the stern to try and make the canoe go where we want." Pashak asked, "Did you ever paddle a canoe before you came north to our land?"

"Not often," admitted Andrew. "A few short trips at Camp Tamogami, but mostly on smooth lakes. I never saw anything like that," he said pointing at the violent frothing river.

"Oh, that will settle down beyond the falls and after the snow water has run off from the river banks."

Andrew got the trader's map out of his pack. He unfolded it and pointed the compass line north toward the place where he had seen the big dipper pointing to the North Star hanging right above the river.

"The river branches into two beyond the falls," said Andrew, looking at the map. "This branch of the river is straight," he said, running his finger along the map toward Fort Chimo. "This other branch that you say the hunters use, it's as curvy as a snake. Look," he said to Pashak. "Look here on the map."

"I don't know too much about maps," said Pashak. "Why do you need a map? You stand up, Andrew, and look down there. Beyond the falls you see the two branches of the river, both flowing north toward Ungava Bay."

Andrew shaded his eyes against the strong spring sunlight and said, "The branch the hunters take has sandbars and fast shallows and white rapids in its curves. The long, straight branch is smooth."

"Yes, it's smooth," said Pashak, "but looks deep and very fast to me. I've never been on that branch of the river. You show old Mium-scum and Agawan your map," said Pashak. "Maybe they will understand it better."

Piwas spread two caribou skins over the gravel outside the tent and they all four lay down to examine the map.

"We're right here at the falls." Pashak first pointed

out the place on the map to Mium-scum, then pointed far north to a star-shaped dot. "That's the way they show Fort Chimo on this piece of paper, and this is the Koksoak River," Pashak shouted above the noise of the falls. He ran his finger along the wildly curving line that twisted like a snake. "The river has these two main branches, one crooked and one straight. Which branch should we take? Androoo wants to know."

Old Mium-scum did not answer right away.

"We take the left branch." He moved his scarred brown finger along its S-shaped curves.

"Ask him," Andrew said, "if he has ever traveled on the right branch of the river."

"No," Mium-scum answered. "None of our people have ever paddled on that branch."

"Well, it looks to me as though that's been their big mistake," said Andrew. "I guess that's because they never had a map. The right branch is almost straight." He reached out and broke off a dwarf willow twig and measured the right river branch against the left. "With all those curves they have to travel almost twice as far to reach Fort Chimo. Ask Agawan if he knew that."

Pashak asked, then shook his head. "He doesn't answer me. Maybe he's just thinking."

"Well," said Andrew, folding up his map, "we're going to go exploring. We're going to paddle down the right branch of the river. It's shorter and it's straighter. You tell him that."

Pashak told Agawan, who just lay there staring along the river in the soft spring light.

Pashak and Andrew stood up for they could hear wild geese calling. As they pointed up to the long wavering wedges of snow geese in the sky, old Mium-scum called out some words to Pashak, who did not translate. Later when they were eating, Andrew asked what the old man had said.

"Oh, nothing much. He only said to tell you that you're not wrong. That the right branch of the river is a lot shorter and less curvy. Oh yes—and he said to tell you that we're going to get a lot faster ride the way you want to go. He says to hold on tight because we are going to fly down that river faster than an arrow!"

Next morning, Pashak said, "You really want to travel on that straight branch of the river?"

"Of course I do," said Andrew. "I believe in maps."

Pashak shook his head. "Androoo, those little black lines on a map don't tell you everything. You should look at the river. Try to understand it. But if you want to go that straight way, I'll try it with you. I'm not afraid of going fast!"

"We've got all the fur baled tight," said Andrew. "Do you think we can get all our things into that one small canoe?"

"Sure we can," said Pashak, "but we won't be doing much jumping around. It's going to be a very bulky load. Mium-scum says he and the others will work down to the place where they left their canoes last autumn on the curvy river."

Everyone walked down to the branching of the river and watched the two boys ease the newly covered canoe into the water, then carefully load all six fur bales and their packs, and food. Andrew and Pashak waved goodbye to everyone.

They pushed off into the river, avoiding the curved

branch, where they could see white water. Andrew
stroked as smoothly as he could, trying not to strike
the canoe's gunwale with his paddle.

"You are a strong paddler," he called back to Pashak
in the stern.

"I am not strong," Pashak answered. "It is the river
that is strong. Even now we are going fast and our
journey has only begun."

What Pashak had said was true. Andrew did not need
to put any strength into his paddle strokes. They only
tried to guide the canoe on a straight course as it
rode swiftly north on the smooth black spring flood of
the river.

By noon they had traveled a long distance. Andrew
did not know how many miles. He got out the map and
said, "At this rate we should reach this place marked
Bad Rock by tomorrow."

"This is really good," called Pashak. "I never went so
fast in a canoe. Our old people are wrong to take that
curvy river branch. It takes too long. I love a good, fast,
easy ride like this."

By midafternoon the river was changing. It was no
longer simply smooth and black and silent. It started
to develop "fish eyes," small whirlpools caused by the
rush of water, and "hay stacks" where white water
thundered angrily against hidden rocks. Far to the
north they could hear a deep-throated roar.

"What's that sound?" said Andrew. "There are no
falls marked on this river."

"I don't know," said Pashak, "but I wonder if we
should paddle into the river bank, make camp and walk
down river to see what's making all that noise?"

"Let's go just a little farther," Andrew said. "If we

can go until sunset and make the same fast run tomorrow, we'll be in Fort Chimo on the third day."

"The true men, the packmen, they would never believe that." Pashak laughed. "Imagine! It took us eleven days of hard-work packing to come inland and less than three days doing nothing to go north again."

"We'll stay fairly close to shore," said Andrew. "That way if the river looks dangerous, we'll head in quickly to the bank."

That sounded safe enough to both of them. But as the late afternoon sun sank low, dark shadows fell across the river, and so hard did Andrew concentrate to see ahead that both he and Pashak failed to notice how much their speed had increased. Suddenly to Andrew's horror he saw a flash of jagged teeth as their canoe slipped over some sharp rocks just below the river's surface. He craned his neck and saw more sharp rocks lurking beneath the water ready to slash the thin bottom of their birch bark canoe.

"Stroke out! Stroke out!" he yelled at Pashak, and together they struggled to work the canoe out toward the center of the river away from the deadly rocks that lurked beneath them.

"Whooh! That was close," cried Andrew, staring down into the dark depths of the rushing river. "We're safe out here."

"Not safe now!" yelled Pashak. "We're in the middle and we're going too fast! Look, look!" he shrieked at Andrew. "That's what makes the roaring. That must be Bad Rock!"

Less than half a mile ahead of them Andrew could see a huge stack of white water churning and beating against a rough rock island in the middle of the river.

"Stroke for the bank," yelled Pashak. "Work hard! Work hard! Stroke, stroke, stroke!" he bellowed.

Andrew dug the blade of his long paddle deep and drew with every ounce of strength that he possessed. They did manage to turn the canoe sideways with its bow pointed almost toward the bank. But the bark canoe, which had no keel, only slithered sideways, caught in the rushing grip of the snow-fed river.

"Stroke! Stroke! Stroke!" Pashak grunted as he put out all his strength.

Andrew could see that they would not make the river bank. "Straighten out. We've got to go straight past that little island, and there's not much space." There were rocks standing out from the river bank causing a white roar of water. And even worse was the spray-lashed island that sent up frightening rainbows in the long rays of evening sunlight.

"I can't keep us straight," yelled Pashak.

But the noise around them was so great that Andrew did not even hear him, and it would not have mattered if he had. The canoe slipped sideways and smashed against the island's rocks. It was torn to pieces, flinging both Andrew and Pashak into the deadly churning waters.

XV

Bad Rock

THE FUR BALES WERE SUCKED BENEATH THE ROARING
white water, then popped to the surface and went ca-
reening down the river. Andrew felt the water flood
into his half of the canoe as it rolled over and went
under. Its ribs cracked and the birchbark tore like
paper. He used the paddle across the gunwales to lever
himself out into the rushing blinding whiteness, and as
he did, he caught a fur bale and clung to it for dear life.
The air trapped in the furs beneath the canvas wrapping caused it to float like a life buoy. He was flung
around in a whirlpool eddy, then slammed into the rock
island. Terror drove him scrambling up over the
smooth, worn rocks with a strength he did not know
he possessed.

He found Pashak lying face down at the foot of the
island's only tree. He was shuddering and gasping,
coughing water from his lungs. Andrew collapsed beside him.

Pashak slowly turned his head and looked around him. "We'd have been better off to drown quick in the river than to lie here soaking wet tonight, slowly freezing to death. No fire, no gun, no fur, no canoe, no nothing," he said to Andrew. "I should have listened to older people who know canoeing. Mium-scum tried to tell us this river was too fast."

"I'd have drowned if I hadn't caught this bale of fur," said Andrew.

"That is something," Pashak admitted, and he felt his belt. The short crooked knife his father had given him was still there.

Pashak slit open the stitched canvas and shook out sixteen tight-packed otter skins.

"They're dry now," he said, "but they won't be that way long unless we can get out of this icy spray."

Pashak stood up and with his crooked knife cut the branches off the small dwarf spruce near him.

It's not an island, it's a bad, bad rock! thought Andrew. It's not much larger than an elephant's back.

Using tree branches and the tough brush growing around the base of the tree, Pashak, with the help of Andrew, tried to build a crude lean-to. Together they spread out half a dozen of the largest otter skins with the fur turned out against the lashing spray.

"They're waterproof," said Pashak as the two of them spread four more pelts on the cold wet stone and huddled inside their shelter. "If we had a fire we could dry ourselves," said Pashak.

"I have matches, but they're soaking wet."

"Let me look at them," said Pashak, and he spread them out on a dry otter pelt. "The matches in the middle are not as wet as all the others. My grandfather told me that he once saw a man dry wet matches in his hair."

"I've heard of that," said Andrew, "but our hair is soaking wet." He shuddered in the growing cold.

"This otter skin is dry," said Pashak, and he started carefully rubbing a single match stick back and forth, going faster and faster until it seemed dry again. "Now I'll dry this stone," he said, rubbing it vigorously across another pelt.

"I'm ready. Can you find any dry twigs?"

"I don't think so," Andrew answered. "Everything on this island is soaking wet with spray."

"Bring me that dead branch off the spruce," said Pashak.

With his crooked knife he cautiously picked away the bark and examined it in the fading light. "This inside bark is dry," he said. "I'll scrape a pile of tinder on the fur. Androoo, you take the canvas and scrub that rock until it's almost dry."

When they were finished, it was nearly dark.

"Bend over close so that no damp spray comes through," said Pashak.

Twice against the dry stone he struck the match before its head fell off.

"It's not going to light," said Andrew, and his teeth were chattering so that he could hardly speak.

"We'll try again," said Pashak. "But it's so dark I can't see now. I don't know which matches are wet or dry. Rub hard behind your ear with your fingers until it's dry. Then hold the matches there. You'll feel if they are wet or dry."

Andrew was surprised to find that he could easily tell. "These two are the best," he said.

Both boys started to rub their matches through the otter fur, drying them with friction. In the darkness Andrew struck his and almost wept when he felt the head give way. Great freezing shudders racked his body and his wet clothing seemed to turn to ice. Then suddenly he saw a small blue sputter that slowly turned into a yellow flame, a match flame! Pashak's match had lit.

Cupping his trembling hands around the precious light, Pashak bent and held it to the tiny tinder pile. The dry bark smoked and smouldered and then caught fire.

"Quickly," said Pashak. "Break off the smallest twigs and toast them dry."

Andrew was surprised to see how well they burned.

"That's because dead spruce is full of sap. You can hear it crackle in the fire. My grandfather says it is the tree's last chance to speak to animals or humans."

"It's a lovely sound," said Andrew as he and Pashak held their numb fingers just above the dancing flames and listened to the wood sap snap.

Welcome heat ran up their arms and down their trembling spines. They added more fuel to the fire and Pashak stripped off his coat and inner shirt and draped a pair of otter skins across his shoulders. He arranged two sticks above the fire and hung his own and Andrew's clothes on them to dry.

"We're not so badly off," said Andrew. "We have shelter and a fire. If only we had something left to eat."

"Eat?" Pashak laughed. "We don't need anything to eat. We can live off our fat for at least two weeks or more, as long as there's plenty of water to drink. What you want to worry about is the wood. Fuel. We will burn up every twig on this miserable rock island in less than two days. After that the wet will creep in again, and then we're finished. If we were on the curving river branch, I'd hope some true men would pass by and see us. But only crazy people like us travel on this killing river!"

"I had a dream," said Andrew, when he woke up in the morning.

"What did you dream?" asked Pashak. "I hope you dreamed that something came to save us."

"No," said Andrew as he blew the fire embers into life and added fuel. He drew the otter skin over his back and shuddered. "The men I saw had bows and arrows and they were trying to shoot us. Kill us."

"So, you saw death in your dreams. That is not surprising," Pashak said.

Andrew felt their coats and leggings. "They're dry enough to put on."

They each tied three otter skins together and made a warm fur shoulder cloak.

"Can't go out," said Pashak. "Too wet out there with all that spray. Nothing to do but lie in here and wait for—wait for nothing!"

On the third day, Pashak spread the canvas bale wrapping over his shoulders and went outside. He screamed at Andrew, "Look! Look! There's a woman. And a child. I think it's Phim. And—and—there's—there's Agawan, and Sango and Piwas, and all the others in that family. Look, they've seen us. They're waving at us. I think I see Wapen and Mium-scum."

He shouted, but, of course, they could not hear his

voice over the awful roar of water crashing against their small rock island.

"They have no canoe," said Andrew.

"Even if they had one, it wouldn't help," said Pashak. "Any canoe would smash to pieces in the rush of water around this rock."

"What are we going to do? Just lie in this wet hut of ours and watch them?"

"Yes," said Pashak, "unless you can think of something else that we should do."

"What's old Mium-scum doing?" Andrew asked.

"I don't know," Pashak answered.

"He's cutting something, making something. Agawan seems to be helping him. Can you guess what they're making?"

"I know what it is," Pashak shouted, and he leaped up so quickly that he nearly knocked their miserable shelter over. "It's a bow and arrow, Androoo. Androoo —your dream. It came true!"

"You mean they're going to shoot us full of arrows?" Andrew snorted.

"No, no. You watch. They're going to try and land an arrow over on this island."

As he spoke, they saw Agawan flex the bow, then Phim handed him an arrow. Agawan raised the bow and aimed at them and shot the arrow. It fell short.

"They're pulling it back again." said Pashak. "They've got a long fishline tied to it."

"What good will that do?" Andrew asked him.

"Look, Mium-scum's going to try it this time."

They saw him aim the bow high into the air and pull it back with all his strength. He released the arrow. It came clattering down onto the stones and stuck into a crack almost at Pashak's feet.

"Oh," said Pashak, snatching up the crude arrow and hugging it to his chest. "This is your dream arrow, Androoo. I never felt so good in all my life."

"Why?" said Andrew.

"You watch," said Pashak, and he took the fishline and gently started to wind it round and round his arm from wrist to elbow. "See what's coming?" he shouted to Andrew, as a long thick strand of sealskin line came snaking through the raging water attached to the end of the thin fishing line.

"I've got it!" Andrew shouted up to Pashak, and he held up the heavy sealskin line in his hands.

"I'll tie it to the tree stump," Pashak said. "I'll tie my best knot. Then you tie yours, Androoo. If our knots give way, we die for sure."

When the line was double tied, they could see old Mium-scum waving to them.

"I go first," said Pashak. "You watch me carefully. And if I make it over, you do just the same. You hear me? If I'm lost—well—goodbye, Androoo. You try it some way different."

He looked at Andrew for a moment, then hooked one arm over the line and held on fast with the other as he forced his way out into the frightening roar of ice cold water. It did not take him long to cross. Andrew saw Sango grab Pashak and haul him to safety on the river bank.

Andrew was about to follow him but turned back. In a moment he had gathered the sixteen otter skins into a loose bundle and lashed them together by the paws.

These he attached to the thin, coiled fishline. Then taking one end of the fishline in his teeth, he flung his arm over the heavy sealskin line. He imitated Pashak, crossing hand over hand in the terrifying rush of water. Fear seemed to give his arms new muscles and before he knew it, he, too, was across and Agawan and Sango and Phim were all pulling him up out of the freezing waters.

"What you got in your mouth?" asked Pashak.

"The fish line," said Andrew.

"Why did you bother with that old fish line?" asked Phim.

"You pull it in and you'll see," gasped Andrew.

When Phim drew the dark bundle of otter skins across the roaring river, Pashak sat down and laughed until the tears rolled down his cheeks.

"Androo, I don't know if we ever make a true man out of you. But I can see that you are going to make a real good Scottish trader!"

XVI

Andrew's Decision

ON SHORE THERE WAS A HUGE BONFIRE BURNING. PHIM and Piwas helped Andrew and Pashak strip off their wet clothes, then wrapped warm wool blankets around their shoulders. But still the two of them shuddered as though the cold had seeped inside their bones.

"What is that they're building?" Andrew asked Pashak, as he pointed to a small tundra sod hut that Osken and Wapen were busy building up against some saplings.

"I hope it is a sweat house," said Pashak, trembling from head to foot. "I can't stop my teeth from chattering."

"Hurry, it's ready now. You two go inside," said Phim.

Andrew followed Pashak, who threw aside his blanket at the entrance. Phim's arm reached after them, handing in a copper kettle full of water.

"It's dark and hot in here." The heat made Andrew gasp.

"Just you wait," said Pashak. He poured some water from the kettle spout onto the fire-blackened stones in the center and a puff of live steam rose, spreading its damp warmth through the sweat house.

"Get ready for some more," said Pashak, and he again poured water on the hot stones.

This time the sweat lodge filled so completely with steam that the two boys could scarcely see each other.

"That feels wonderful," Andrew said, as he sat down on a short log and relaxed in the steaming heat.

Pashak raised his arms and stretched. "I'm trying to forget the days and nights in that cold, wet hut on Bad Rock. We're lucky to be alive and safe. I wonder how they ever found us?"

After they had scrubbed down from the little sweat house and put on their fire-dried clothes, Pashak asked Agawan.

"It was your sisters, Phim and Wapen, who saved you," Agawan answered.

The others explained. "Not long after you two had gone down the straight fast arm of the river, Mium-scum and Agawan decided we should leave, following the slower, curvy branch. Even it was moving far too fast. On our third night out, we stopped and slept, and in the early morning, when the air was still, we could hear a distant rumbling.

" 'What's that sound?' Wapen asked us.

" 'A waterfall maybe,' Mium-scum answered them. 'The straight branch is not so far from this bend of our river.'

"Both your sisters pleaded with us to wait while they

ran over to the falls, saying that they were worried about your safety. In the end, almost everyone decided to go."

"I thought Mium-scum and Wapen would still be too weak to make the journey," Agawan said. "So I set out with Piwas, Sango and Phim and their children following. We pulled our canoes up high and parted from the others. Together we walked across the land. It is not so far.

"When we arrived, we saw it was not a waterfall we had heard but water pounding against that rough rock island. Phim was the first to see you two stranded there. It was then that Mium-scum and Wapen joined us."

After Pashak and Andrew had eaten, Agawan said, "If you feel well enough to travel, we could start out now and walk back. We could reach our canoes on the curving river before the weather changes."

And so they did, with Andrew and Pashak trying to make their cramped legs keep up to all the others. Phim carried the sixteen otter skins that she had carefully dried for Andrew. Some skins had been singed, but most remained lustrous pelts.

When they reached Mium-scum's tent and the canoes, they ate again and slept. This time Andrew dreamed that he saw a graceful young woman appear and aim an arrow at him. But when she released it, it turned into a beautiful many-colored bird that soared above his head toward the sun. He woke up thinking of his own sister and of his mother and his father. How lucky I am, he thought, to feel so sure that they're not starving.

In the morning they loaded the canoes and set out early. Andrew did not tell Pashak of his dream, fearing that old Mium-scum might hear of it and tell him what it meant. The four canoes were greatly overcrowded, with long-legged Andrew and his otter pelts doubled up in one and Pashak jammed inside another.

Andrew noticed that none of the adults paddled the canoes but sat back talking and enjoying the slowly changing scenery as the four children did more than their share of work. That evening when they landed, and the women and children were putting up the tents and gathering firewood and water, Andrew asked Pashak why the young ones did so much.

"How else will they learn unless they paddle the canoes, haul water, build the fires, and set up tents? That is the way our people teach the children. Here we have always raised both boys and girls to help their elders. Is that not so in your country, Androoo?"

"Long ago I think it was like that," said Andrew, "but now everything has changed."

"Everything is changing with us, too," said Pashak. "My grandfather Natiwapio and Mium-scum and even Agawan all say they don't like the way the changes are coming so quickly. Mium-scum said last night that white people like to race down long, straight, dangerous rivers and maybe break up everything. We true men prefer this slow and curving river. Is it not beautiful?" he said, waving his hand toward the far bank covered with lush caribou moss.

Andrew looked at it with new eyes now that the winter snows had melted, turning everything gray-green in the warm spring sunlight. A huge flock of snow geese rose into the air, circling, calling to others before they formed a long, loose wedge and headed north toward their Arctic nesting grounds.

"We are like those geese," said Pashak. "In autumn we journey south into the forests to seek our winter food. When spring comes again, we return to the barrens to do our summer trading and to meet with all our people, to feast with them and dance, and find husbands and wives for the young people. We sing songs and tell of all the strange things that have happened to us. We gabble together just like geese."

Andrew lay back in the canoe on the following day and watched the birds and animals along the banks and the smooth sweep of the river as it curved north toward the mist-hung vastness of Ungava Bay. He watched the big red-bellied trout leap into the air and snatch at flies.

They made camp early, and while the children helped the women build an outdoor fire, the men set out a gill net for fish. Just at dark they saw a canoe prow moving into the firelight.

"It's Cut Cheek." The children shrieked and ran behind their parents when they saw the strange symbols of monsters, moons and stars painted on the bow of his canoe. In this way Cut Cheek rejoined them as they went toward the fort.

The morning brought a fair breeze blowing at their backs. Agawan said that if it continued, they should reach their journey's end before evening.

Andrew and Pashak and some others helped the children paddle for they were eager to arrive. Just at sunset they rounded the last bend in the river and before them on the right bank they could see Fort Chimo.

Old Mium-scum raised his gun and fired it in the air. Agawan laughed aloud and fired his from the second canoe, and Andrew watched Cut Cheek land and scrub

the mystical symbols from the bow of his canoe and
change his magic shirt for something plain.

"Why's he doing that?" called Andrew.

"Most white people don't believe in magic," Pashak
said. "Our magic men make them nervous. You better
not tell them how you dreamed we were saved by bow
and arrow. They don't like talk like that!"

Cut Cheek rejoined them, but now all his face paint
was gone and he seemed like any ordinary hunter.

"Look!" screamed Phim.

From the fort, Andrew saw a thick cloud of white
smoke belch out and roll along the river. It was some
time before they heard the echoing boom.

"They see us," cried Piwas. "They fired the cannon.
Now everyone must be getting ready. Look at them
running down to the landing to see our canoes arrive."

"Stop paddling," Pashak called to Andrew. "Give
your paddle to that little girl. It looks bad if full-grown
men like us have to paddle into Chimo. Sit back. Enjoy
the scenery and the fort. We haven't seen anything like
this for more than seven moons!"

There were at least sixty men, women and children
down at the landing to greet them. When they drew
near, Andrew recognized Pashak's grandfather Natiwapio first, for he was taller than all the rest. Then he
saw Nakasuk, the Eskimo, with many of his relatives,
all in their sealskin boots and high, white, pointed
hoods. Old Dougal came hurrying down from the factor's house wearing his best red tam upon his head. Andrew saw Pashak's mother and dozens of other smiling
faces that he recognized. They, too, had returned to the
trading post from their inland journeys. It was almost
like coming home.

When he stepped out of the canoe and stretched his legs, he heard a familiar voice call out, "Well, I'm glad to see you all back here safe and sound!"

It was the factor, Alistair McFee, grinning broadly, shaking hands with all of them.

"We didn't get the outpost finished and I lost almost all the fur, sir. We—"

"Well, never mind that, Andrew Stewart," the factor said. "I'm going to enjoy the fact that you and Pashak and these Naskapi families are safely home again. From what I've heard of this winter's hardships inland, it's a miracle that you're all alive. I sent two packmen back to Ghost Lake with food. But you had disappeared, your tracks blown in with snow. They tried, but could not follow you. Sometimes here we feared the worst. But that's all over now."

"I've only this one bundle of otter skins," said Andrew.

"Well, that's not too bad," the factor answered. "Otter prices are sky-high this year. We heard that on the radio from Montreal. Oh yes, and we heard as well that George's back is strong again, but he's gone back to school."

"Good," Pashak said. "Tomorrow, when Andrew goes into the store, he's going to get a big surprise." Saying no more he walked off happily with his family.

Andrew ate a huge meal in the trader's house and heard all their winter news. When he got into bed, he seemed to hang down in its springy softness, and he was too hot and could not go to sleep. Finally he climbed out of the bed, rolled himself in a thick woolen blanket and went to sleep on the good hard, rough floor.

Andrew woke when he heard a tapping at his window and at first he could not remember where he was.

"Androoo, why you sleeping on the floor? You trying to turn into a real true man? Have you given up sleeping in soft white beds forever?"

Andrew jumped up and looked out at Pashak, who had on a bright new hat his mother had made for him.

"Come on," he said, pointing at his hat. "She's making one for you, too. She'll give it to you later. My grandfather's got something he wants to say to all of us. You, too. Hurry!" Pashak said as Andrew dressed himself.

When they entered Pashak's family tent, it was crowded with people. Pashak translated what his grandfather Natiwapio was saying.

"We true people who remain alive have seen a long, hard winter. We are the fortunate ones," said Natiwapio. "All that is past is past. Be thankful all of you that we here still have breath.

"We are like the sacred animals who give us their flesh that we may live. We are born and are cared for by our parents, who in their turn grow old. Then the children repay the kindness of their mother and their father and older relatives by caring for them. That is the way life goes with us. We are all of us like the moon, born into the night sky as a thin, curved, sliver of light that slowly grows into a bright full moon then slowly wanes as it grows old and disappears, only to be reborn again like an infant who appears with a face and ways just like his relatives. And yet, this newborn infant remembers nothing of its past."

Pashak was careful to repeat and explain to Andrew every word that the old man had spoken.

"I have never thought of life in just that way," said Andrew. "I will not forget what Natiwapio has said."

"My family asks you as a son to sleep here with all of us tonight. My mother says that she is eager to have you here because she knows that soon—this summer or next—you will leave us to return to help take care of your real parents."

Next day when Andrew and Pashak stepped inside the store, they saw Alistair McFee standing behind the counter and a dozen hunters waiting to trade.

"They say you've had a good late season's trapping," said Alistair McFee to Andrew.

"I told you, sir, that everything went wrong with us. I didn't get the outpost built, and because I believed the thin lines on a map and not the wisdom of these people, I almost drowned Pashak and myself. When our canoe was wrecked, I lost five bales of fur. I failed. We brought back almost nothing."

"That's not so," said Pashak. "All these men say they were our hunting companions—the packmen and those from Agawan's and Mium-scum's camps. They say this is our share of the winter's catch."

The hunters laughed and cast a pile of furs out onto the center of the floor.

"You didn't fail," the trader said to Andrew. "You and Pashak cached the trade goods on Ghost Lake exactly as you said you would. You've earned enough to pay your passage south this summer. I guess after the hard winter that you've suffered you'll be glad to hurry back to school."

"No," said Andrew. "I'm not ready to go back to school just yet. Especially after this morning. I owe all these true men fur. They taught me how to live inland and survive. Now, if Pashak's willing and . . .

if you'll allow *us* . . . we'll go back when the river freezes and finish building the outpost on Ghost Lake, and I'll pay back all my debts."

Pashak laughed and said, "Androoo, you haven't got any debts with us. True men, they don't think that way."

During the afternoon Andrew wrote a long letter to his family, which the ship would take back when it paid its summer visit. He told them about his winter inland and that he would remain in the north for a second year as they had planned for him if he wanted to. He said that he would return home the following summer and go back to school that autumn. Andrew knew that those words would please his parents and he, too, felt pleased to have a firm plan in his mind.

In mid-June the mosquitoes rose from the swamp behind the fort in stinging hordes, marking the true beginning of the short subarctic summer. The charter ship arrived with a new apprentice from Newfoundland. Pashak and Andrew tried to teach him what they knew. Each day Andrew did all he could to learn to speak Naskapi. Many people gladly helped him.

With the coming of the autumn moon, a time of plenty returned to them. The hunters brought in fresh caribou and plump geese and heavy silver salmon, and the true men held a feast with drumming and singing and laughing and eating until the hunters and their families nearly burst. In the middle of the feasting, Pashak's mother gave a splendid many-colored hat to Andrew.

"My mother says our family wants to adopt you for their son," Pashak explained. "That way you'll be my brother, and Wapen and Phim will be your sisters. That will make us all one family. Our grandfather gives you your new name—*Miam T'chin*. It means *fine man*."

Andrew thanked his new mother and his grandfather. He noticed that his hands were not quite steady when he placed the splendid gift hat upon his head because of his great pleasure and deep excitement.

"Our grandfather is going to sing a song he made for you, and while he sings, my mother's going to feed you," said Pashak.

The old man began in a high and quavering voice. Each time he spoke Andrew's new name, he struck the drum.

"I have a grandson, a fine man named *Miam T'chin*.
The blood of my veins flows toward
My new son *Miam T'chin*.
I have a good son who shares with others,
My fine son *Miam T'chin*.
I have a son who respects the rushing river,
My wise son *Miam T'chin*.
I have a son who hears the animals singing,
Oh yes, he hears their sacred singing,
My grandson *Miam T'chin*."

When his adoption song was over, Andrew rose and left the tent. He walked far along the river bank alone. The autumn was upon them, and the sky was once more growing dark at night. In the southwest Andrew could see the Dog Star flickering like one bright candle in the blackness. High above his head the northern lights appeared and sent their long, pale fingers probing down toward the earth. All the land to the south seemed to slope into dark tundra plains, as the Aurora

Borealis glowed in the night sky, mirrored in the curving river.

Far away inland Andrew heard the first faint sound of a wolf as it sent up its long and lonesome howling. He breathed deeply, shuddered with pleasure and wrapped his arms around himself to hold out the night chill that came seeping up from the water. Behind him from the big Naskapi tent he heard the muffled rhythm of the drum and the sound of human voices singing. When the wolves called again, these two distinct sounds seemed to blend into one as though the singers and the wolves were calling, speaking to each other, as though the languages of all the animals and humans had become a part of the land, a part of each other. Andrew raised up his arms in joy. He felt as though he, too, had become a part of everything upon this earth.

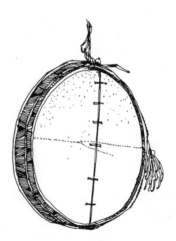